Stealing Squatch

SAVANNA GOLDEN

ISBN: 979-8-9914457-2-6

Imprint: Independently Published

Cover design by: Savanna Golden via Canva

Character art commissioned from: M.T Zimny

Printed in the United States of America

This book is dedicated to the early readers of Mate Match. You believed in me even when I wasn't sure of myself. You requested Alder and Kai's story, so here it is. Thank you for being a part of this journey.

—Love, Savanna

Celeste Blackmore's Playlist

Bad Witch Energy

Contents

One

KAI

Sprinting forward, I jumped between the two adolescent boys who were trading violent blows. I pushed between their bodies to separate them. It took a considerable amount of strength to stop the punch that came from the one on my left. I caught the punch that headed for the other boy's gut.

The girl who called me was crying frantically on the sidelines, clutching the hem of her shirt in a tight fist as she begged them to stop.

"Please! Quit fighting. Don't hurt each other," she implored them as tears continued to follow the wet path already flowing down her cheeks.

Despite my shove, they tried to continue exhibiting aggression toward each other. It wasn't until I released a roar of anger that they separated. The power and authority of the sound forced them apart as they recognized a stronger, more powerful wolf amongst them.

"Explain yourselves," I commanded.

The one with the shaggy hair told me that he found out his "woman" was going behind his back with the lanky one. The lanky one insisted it was the other way around. The girl who'd stopped crying stepped forward at the accusations, insisting that neither of them were being completely honest.

"I'm not dating either of these idiots. They just both seem to think they have some type of claim on me. Charles, we shared one kiss, like a month ago. Brett took me to the movies the other night on a date and that pissed Charles off." She huffed in frustration before crossing her arms.

The lanky one who was apparently Charles spoke up, "That's not fair Carly, you know we have something going on. You shouldn't have gone to the movies with him." This was accompanied by an accusing finger point in the direction of Brett.

Brett's jaw clenched as he spoke, "Just cause a girl kisses you, *one time*, doesn't make her your girlfriend."

He had a point, but Charles didn't seem to agree. He took a menacing step in the direction of his rival.

"Back up," I told him with a force.

He stopped but he didn't back away as I asked him to.

"Carly and Brett, go home," I told them. "Charles, stay where you're at. We have things to discuss."

I waited for the two I dismissed to leave. They hadn't done anything wrong.

Once they walked away, I turned and told Charles, "Girls can change their minds about you. You could be in a relationship for real, not just a perceived one, and they can still change their mind. At any point, someone can change their mind, and you can't go attacking anyone who they start seeing."

Now that the other two were gone, the cloud of anger around him had disappeared. His face had patches of red, marring his tanned skin, and his brown eyes looked suspiciously glossy.

"I just really thought we had something special," he choked out. His throat worked on a swallow like he had a tightness there, trying to control his emotions.

"I know, bud. I'm sorry it didn't work out. It hurts now, but this pain won't last forever. Someday, you'll find someone you'll connect with on an even deeper level, and you won't even remember this." I didn't bother to tell him my thoughts on mating bonds; instead, I put away my pessimistic views on love to comfort him.

"Yeah, I hope you're right."

I gave him a pat on the shoulder and sent him on his way.

Later that night I sat in the study with my feet on the desk. The ice clanked against the glass as I took another sip of the whiskey. The liquid burned my throat as it went down, and I savored the feeling.

Dealing with those kids earlier ended up being the least stressful of my day's work tasks. Everything after was more complex and came with higher risks.

Taking another sip of whiskey, I thought over the last six months. Everything that happened has changed all our lives—mostly for the better—but also shifted us all into new roles.

Our pack used to be led by Angus MacGregor, whose family had been leading it for several generations. When he passed away, leaving the commanding position open, all three of his sons participated in a challenge to determine a new alpha. His middle son Fallon won the challenge against his older brother Callum and younger brother Knox.

The power quickly went to Fallon's head, and he started behaving like a dictator. It's expected for any pack alpha to be mated, and since he wasn't, he was required to choose a mate. Things hit the fan when he announced to the entire pack that Finley was his choice for mate.

Finley had no desire to be mated to Fallon for multiple reasons. For starters, they had a complicated history. They were best friend growing up. They started drifting apart when Finley started dating Fallon's brother Callum and eventually became engaged to him. Their relationship ended after Finley caught him cheating on her, and Fallon turned his back on her in the worst way. Before the announcement, she'd also started dating a warlock named Xan, who turned out to be her fate's blessed mate.

When Fin publicly turned Fallon down, he became unhinged and abducted Xan. Obviously, my girl and I wouldn't stand for it. We swooped in and rescued the trouble-making warlock—okay, we had some help from Xan's close circle of friends.

Until Finley met Xan, we primarily surrounded ourselves with other wolf shifters. Now, we are a tight-knit group that also includes a dark, broody vampire, a satyr with golden retriever energy, a light fairy who can make anyone feel joy, and, unfortunately, a squatch.

We went on our little rescue mission into the woods, ready to battle to retrieve Xan, only to find out Fallon's brothers released him. The three of them were already in the process of leaving the cabin.

We regrouped, and since the pack was hunting us, we hid. Xan owns a creepy Victorian mansion in the middle of nowhere called the Wimbleton Estate. The place was essentially a death trap, but it was spacious. Beggars can't be choosers, so we made do.

We bided our time while gathering allies and forming a coup. The only way to remove an alpha from power is for someone else to challenge them in a fight. The challenger must either force their opponent to submit, forfeiting the fight, or kill them.

It's a brutal process in theory, and it wasn't much better to watch.

We argued a bit at first when we discussed who should throw down the gauntlet. Neither of the other MacGregor boys wanted to take their brother on, and I sure didn't want to. In the end, I suggested Finley. She was a stronger wolf than any of us, and her anger fueled her.

Conditions in the pack deteriorated significantly during the few weeks we were in hiding. Fallon completely lost his mind, even forcing the pack to camp in his family's backyard so he could monitor everyone. Some people lost their jobs because he wouldn't allow them to leave. He grew increasingly aggressive and tyrannical.

The pack practically gave a collective sigh of relief when Finley came in like an avenging angel to a duel.

Things were not well between them with their shared history, but she still didn't really want to kill him. During the fight, she tried to get him to submit rather than the alternative. He refused, and ultimately, Finley had to put him down to protect the pack.

I know it hurt her to end her former best friend, but she knew it was for the good of the pack.

With Finley, the new leader, she made some changes that were monumental for not just the pack but the supernatural world. She made history by opening our pack to include other species of supernaturals. No one had ever done that before; for the most part, reactions have been okay. We still must deal with the occasional consequence of that choice, but the fallout could have been much worse.

When the position of power transitioned, I was appointed as Finley's second. I had readily accepted the position, willing to do anything to support my bestie. Usually, my position as second in command, the pack enforcer, didn't bother me too much. But other days like today made me miss my old life.

Taking another sip of my whiskey, I thought back over the last six months and what a wild time it's been.

ALDER

I knew I was daydreaming again, but I couldn't bring myself to break free of its grip. It was the same as always. It was not a true dream, but a memory of the time passion bubbled over, and my fate-blessed mate gave in to me physically.

Kai was the type of take-charge woman who knew what she wanted and was determined to pursue it. Unfortunately, the reverse was also true: She knew what she didn't want, particularly me.

When my best friend Alexander was abducted by an alpha wolf who was practically feral, everyone in his friend group banded together with his mate to get him back. That was the first time I laid eyes on her. To say she was unimpressed would be putting it mildly. But my heart wouldn't back down, feeling as if it wanted to leap from my chest at just the sight of her. I often had to remind myself she didn't want me, and my squatch didn't like that much.

She only spoke to me to bicker or try and push me away. But one night, barely over six months ago, she broke.

We were all in hiding from the deranged alpha of the Fang pack, staying at a run-down Victorian mansion owned by Xan while we planned our coup. While the manor was large, there were nine of us living there. The place felt crowded, and adjusting to feeling like someone was always underfoot took considerable time.

Finley, Xan's mate, and Kai's best friend, asked for her and me to clean the library room so it could be used as our meeting room. We spent most of the day ignoring each other as we went through the things in the room, throwing stuff away, wiping stuff down, etc. But I'd had enough at some point, and I started baiting her back.

I was just reveling in the memory of her hands on my body when a throat cleared behind me. Startled I had to toss down the nail gun I'd been using to stop myself from falling off the roof of the cabin.

I turned my head and locked eyes with Callum. He raised his hands in a surrender motion and gave me a sheepish smile.

He only joined our group recently. The dark-haired wolf shifter had a complicated past. Several years ago, he and Finley were engaged to be married—which was kind of unusual since shifters and many other supernaturals chose to create a mate bond rather than marry. While they were attending separate colleges, Finley caught him cheating on her. They broke up and hadn't been on speaking terms until the coup.

Callum was the older brother of Fallon, the feral alpha that led the Fang pack for a short time. During the tyranny of Fallon's reign, Callum and the youngest brother, Knox, joined our group to overthrow him.

"Sorry, man. Didn't mean to startle you. I called your name when I approached the cabin, but you were in your own world."

I sighed, knowing he was right. I was in my own little world, thinking about my girl.

"So, you're still set on doing this?" He gestured at the cabin I was currently building. It wasn't much to look at yet, but I was determined to build the perfect sanctuary here, away from the main house for privacy but close enough to get there quickly if there was an emergency. I've been working for months on building this special place just for us in between helping with repairs to the main house.

I ignored him temporarily, choosing to remain quiet. Once again, I picked up the nail gun and started shooting nails into the shingles as I attached them to the roof.

Under his scrutinizing stare, my face flushed. I started feeling too hot and had to remove my long flannel sleeve to continue working in my undershirt.

"Why are you building this cabin for her? She's made her stance clear on your bond." He used a softened tone probably to try and lessen the blow of rejection I felt from my mate. But it still hurt. But my heart, heavy with longing, still hurt.

"She feels crowded in that house with everyone staying there. I want her to be comfortable and happy. It's not about the bond. My squatch doesn't like me sitting back and doing nothing. He insistently yammers inside my head about how we must provide for our mate."

Make mate happy. My squatch grumbled in my mind.

What do you think I'm doing this for? I grumbled back.

"Damn. That must be rough." He ran his hand through his hair, adjusting his stance.

Things started out on a bad note when he first joined our group; no one trusted him, and there were things he and Finley needed to discuss to get closure. After these last few months, things had gotten significantly better. He found his place with us though he was still scared shitless sometimes of Fin's mate Xan. I think that had to do with Xan being a warlock, and he was convinced he would end up hexed or cursed in the first few weeks of living with us.

Finley, being the new alpha, put a stop to anyone giving him too hard of a time, but Xan was so wrapped around her finger that he wouldn't have done anything she would disapprove of.

"Well, as much as I feel this is pointless, do you want a hand?"

I didn't mind Callum so much, and since there was still a lot to be done, I accepted his help.

"I won't be able to finish all of this tonight, and it's supposed to rain. There is a tarp down there. Can you lay it out on the other side of the roof?" I pointed to the side I wouldn't finish.

"Sure, whatever you need."

We fell into companionable silence as we worked. When I finished nailing shingles on my side of the roof, he was just finishing strapping down the tarp.

"You going to work on this again tomorrow?" He asked me.

"Yep."

We climbed down the ladder and headed to the main house to join our friends for our communal dinner. Along the way, he said, "I'll be here to help."

Three

KAI

I was in the office, buried in reports I'd received from some of the wolves who watch the pack boarders, reading over their notes, when Leora poked her pale head into the room.

She smiled that beaming smile she often wore and said, "Family dinner is ready."

I sighed before I tossed the report I'd been reviewing onto the desk and stood. I was starving, so hearing that the food was ready was excellent. I just would've preferred if I could've eaten it in solitude. For the most part, I enjoyed the family dinners, as we called them. Our inner circle of close friends would gather almost every night to eat our dinner. It was great for camaraderie. Unfortunately, it meant I had to be in the presence of the one person I tried my hardest to avoid—the squatch-shaped one.

I followed Leora as we walked down the hallway towards the formal dining room. As we walked, I couldn't help but catalog our differences. She was this petite light fairy with whitish blond hair, always happy and graceful. I, on the other hand, was a moody bitch half the time, and my version of gracefulness was stomping along in my biker boots.

When we entered the dining room, it appeared we were the last ones to get there; everyone else was already seated around the table.

Leora practically danced her way to the open seat next to her mate Ry, the satyr of our group. When she got within two feet of him, her skin started glowing, which happened when she was happy, which was practically all the time.

I took the last open seat, which, thankfully, was between Knox and Hadeon. In the past, I've made a point to clarify my seating preference; I didn't want to be stuck sitting next to Alder. Everyone liked to give me crap about my aversion to him; he is basically a giant-sized man with the strongest golden retriever energy anyone could contain. They didn't get it, but they also didn't know what we were to each other. So, they didn't understand why I spent all my time avoiding him. Fine by me. Honestly, they could stay guessing. I haven't even told Finley about it, and she's my best friend. Nope, I would take that information to my grave.

Tossing myself into my seat with a grunt, I settled in for the meal.

A ding noise indicated that the warmer's timer had gone off. Alder, who was closest to the warmer, jumped up and grabbed the bag.

"Here," he yelled before tossing it across the table.

His aim was off as the red blob was flung in my direction. Eyes closed tight, I braced myself to be covered in blood, but before it could hit me in the face, a hand shot out, grabbing it midair.

"Thanks, man," Hadeon told him before stabbing a straw into the plastic and taking a long draw from the blood within.

I wrinkled my nose as I looked between them.

Firstly, what the heck? Alder's aim sucks. If Hadeon wasn't a vampire, that bag of blood probably would have hit me in the face. I don't know the strength of the plastic bags, but the last thing I want is blood to get all over me, disgusting. Secondly, I wasn't sure I would ever get used to a vampire drinking blood at the dinner table. Like, I get it, but still.

After that, the roast was passed along, followed by the vegetables and the most delicious mashed potatoes ever. We were all stuffing food in our faces, some of us talking quietly until Xan cleared his throat.

"So, listen," he started, "Finley and I have plans tonight, and I'm going to need everyone to stay out of the woods."

Knox scrunched his eyebrows in confusion. "Why can't we be in the woods?"

Finley, sitting at the head of the table, visibly flushed, her cheeks going bright red.

Xan answered, "I've been working on a tonic that I'm hoping hides scent trails. We're going to try it out." He waggled his eyebrows at the group. "Fin's going to hunt me in the woods."

Knox, still unable to understand, says, "Oh, cool. But why can't we be in the woods? That shouldn't mess with your test."

Alder groaned in anticipation of what was coming; internally, I was in solidarity.

"Because if and when she finds me, she'll get a reward." A huge grin slides across his face just thinking of it. "And nothing against you guys, but I don t need any of you seeing my mate naked. So..." He trailed off, and I saw when Knox got it.

"You're going to get busy in the woods?" He asked incredulously.

"Wouldn't be the first time." Xan winked at him.

"Oh, fates. Yuck, stop." I complained. "We don't all want to know about your sex life."

"Why, because yours is sexless?" He asked with an innocent face.

"That's not—" I started to tell him it wasn't true. But he wasn't wrong. I used to use Mate Match—the paranormal dating app—to meet people. More with hookups in mind than relationships. My use of the app is how Finley ended up meeting Xan. She wanted to try dating, and I bullied her into making a profile while we were out drinking.

Like I said, I used to frequently use the app, but that was before I met the insufferable squatch sitting across the table. When we met, I knew very quickly he was my fate's blessed mate. I tried to push him away, to avoid him at all costs, but I failed. We ended up hooking up when we were in hiding here at the estate before Finley challenged Fallon MacGregor for control of Fang pack.

Since then, I've tried a few times to go out with someone to have a little fun, but I just couldn't do it. The idea of being with anyone but him made my stomach sour, even though I didn't want to be with him.

As a child, I saw too much of the bad that can happen when you have a mate, and I wanted nothing to do with it.

CALLUM

I had been cutting it close on time to get to the cabin. I shifted and ran there in my wolf form to avoid keeping my squatchy friend waiting. When I arrived, it was exactly our meet-up time. The only problem was that Alder wasn't there.

Retreating to the tree coverage, I changed back to my human form before sitting on the cabin porch and waiting.

The problem was that after ten minutes of waiting, the squatch still wasn't there. It was all very unlike him. I might be a newer member of this ragtag crew, but Alder has been one of the more welcoming members, so I've gotten to know him well. This means I know he's never late for anything.

I slipped my phone out of my pocket and tried to call him. It rang repeatedly until I reached the voicemail message.

"It's Callum, and we said we'd be meeting to finish that roof. I'm at the cabin. Call me back." I hung up.

Pacing the length of the porch, I waited a little longer. I texted him when I didn't get called back after another ten minutes.

> Hey, are we still working on the roof?

After a few more minutes, I decided to get started without him; surely, he'd be on his way soon.

I uncovered the unfinished section and started nailing the shingles like I saw Al do yesterday. When I had finished, I looked around, realizing that hours had passed, and I was still alone. Grabbing my phone, I checked to see if I had received any messages, but there were none.

Well, whatever, maybe something important came up.

The sun was starting to go down, so I knew it was almost family dinner time. I put away the materials and tools and headed back to the estate.

My timing was excellent, and I got back just as a tasty-smelling pasta dish was set on the dining table. I walked into the room and took a big whiff of the steaming garlic bread. That's practically kryptonite to me, so I groaned and savored it.

Grabbing a chair, I sat down as the others came in. The vampire Hadeon ended up sitting on one side of me and my brother Knox on the other.

"You stink, wolf," Hadeon glared my way. "You heard of the invention of this thing called a shower?" He kept a completely straight face as he asked. It was hard as fuck to read him. I could never tell if he was teasing me or trying to provoke me. Were all vampires so expressionless, or just this one? I haven't ever met any vamps other than him.

"It's not my fault. I told Alder I'd help him with a construction project today, but he never showed up. I had to do twice the work." I wasn't peeved about working on the roof since it kept me busy, but I did worry about Al, one of my only friends here.

He narrowed his eyes for a second, almost seeming to judge whether I was being truthful or not. Whatever. I knew I was still earning the trust of this group.

The food started being passed around, and I filled my plate, happy to stuff myself full. Shifters tend to eat more than normal humans, and I was starving; my plate would probably equate to that of three humans.

Around a chunk of the cheesy garlic bread, I asked, "Speaking of Alder, has anyone seen him?" Glancing around the room, seeing his seat still empty was concerning. Just like he was never late, he also never skipped out on family dinners.

Everyone denied seeing or hearing from Al, except for Xan, who was the only one to see him today. "He went to town this morning to run some errands. That was before breakfast, and he mentioned he would stop at that little café on the square before attending to his other tasks."

"Do you know where else he was going?" Hadeon asked.

"Hmm, no. He didn't say."

Hadeon pulled his phone from his pocket and started rapidly typing. Did that crazy vampire have trackers or something on all of us? I wouldn't put it past him.

He paused, head tilted before he put his phone back into his pocket.

When he said nothing about his findings, Xan asked, "Well, what's going on?"

"He's fine," was the only reply.

Finley looked at Hadeon questioningly, but the vampire just went back to drinking blood from a coffee mug, not meeting anyone's eyes. She took out her phone, too, and started scrolling.

She gasped, the color blanching slightly from her face. She tried to stuff her phone away, but Kai stole it first.

The mood in the room shifted. The level of hostility changed the feel of the air. We wolves picked up easier on strong emotions than others, so the air felt sticky and uncomfortable.

"Who is that?" She whispered the kind of whisper that was a precursor to bad things to come.

The rest of us moved, forming a half circle behind Kai, trying to get a look.

Finley had pulled up the Pack Room, the world's most popular social media for supernaturals to keep in touch. On the screen was a photo Alder was tagged in at the cafe. That wasn't the issue. The problem was he wasn't alone in the photo. A very petite woman with blue hair and black glasses was sitting on his lap. He was smiling ear to ear while the mystery woman kissed his cheek.

"What is Celeste doing here, and why is she with Alder?" Alexander mused out loud.

"Who is Celeste?" If no one else was going to ask, I didn't mind being on the chopping block; I was too nosy not to ask.

"My cousin—last I knew, she lived in Georgia—I've not heard anything about her coming to town. Truthfully, she's bad news, and I would've preferred never to cross paths with her again." He seemed to visibly shiver at the thought.

If Xan, who is not only a warlock but also tends to fall on the side of morally questionable, says this woman is bad news, this cannot be a good sign. What's she capable of that scares him?

"This doesn't sound good." Knox said, stating the obvious.

"Nothing good ever comes of being near Celeste."

After everyone was done gawking at the photo, we ate mostly in silence, except Kai, who stalked from the room, slamming the front door as she left. Kai thought we didn't know what they were to each other, but Alder told us in confidence.

As I chewed a mouthful of pasta, I kept thinking about Al being with Celeste, and no matter how I turned it around, I just couldn't make sense of it. He was so dedicated to the idea of convincing Kai he could be a good mate for her. He had these long-range plans to woo the cranky wolf. So why was he with Celeste? And according to Xan, who hasn't seen Celeste in decades, they don't know each other as far as he knows. So how did they meet? The whole thing was confusing and starting to stress me out.

That night, as I laid down for bed, I tossed and turned; there was a bad feeling in my gut that I just couldn't shake.

Five

CELESTE

Two weeks on the road hadn't done me any favors. When I fled Georgia, I didn't have time to go back home and grab clothes, toiletries, or other personal items. Luckily, I had a spelled bag full of my potions, magical ingredients, and copies of my favorite grimoires.

I had been at a customer's house doing a very rare and complex spell when I got an alert that the wards around my property had been breached. When I scried to see who was at my home, I was met with the scene of a task force descending on it.

I'd been skirting the laws of the International Bureau of Magical Enforcement for many years. But I had always stayed one step ahead of them, hiding my identity.

Guessing from the group who were going through all my belongings it was clear my time was up.

The customer I was working for not only didn't get a job completed, but I also erased their memory of the encounter and stole their car.

When I left the state, I stopped at a truck stop and traded the stolen car for a different one.

Initially, I was unsure where to go; I just drifted around. Then, at one of the rest stops, I was doom scrolling my feed on Pack Room while I waited for a sandwich I ordered for lunch. I was mindlessly scrolling when I came across a photo my cousin Alexander uploaded with his mate and a group of friends.

I hadn't talked to Alexander in years. Our mothers were sisters, but they couldn't have been more different. My mother tended to like darker magic, whereas he liked using magic for good, as if magic was all unicorns and rainbows. Gag me.

Even though he was raised by a mother who chose to use magic for good, Alexander was more like me. He didn't drift toward as dark of magic, but he wasn't all about the moral high road either.

With the invention of the website Ancestral Grimoire, which allowed families to add spells, potion recipes, rituals, etc., to a shared online family grimcire, I was able to see that he was heavily into hexes and curses.

I did not feel compelled to act quickly, so I looked at the profiles of all the people tagged in that photo Alexander had posted.

They seemed like they might not be the smartest bunch. None of their profiles were set to private, so I spent hours scrolling through each of their pages, reading their comments and posts.

One of them stood out to me. His name was Alder Waldvogel. His profile listed him as a sasquatch, though there were no photos of him in his natural form. He was attractive and looked like a very large, rugged man with wavy brown hair and dark green eyes that reminded me of the forest.

The photos he posted and the ones he was tagged in tell a story of an all-around friendly, well-liked guy who seemed to always be smiling.

The more photos I saw of him, the more I wanted to climb this giant like a tree.

My magic almost felt like a purr in my chest as I sat back finishing my sandwich, watching a video of him with his friends.

With his profile set to public, I could see that his location was Silver Ridge, West Virginia, the same town as my cousin's.

I decided what better place to go than to pay my estranged cousin a visit and try and connect with the handsome squatch.

So that's what I did. Now, I'd been in town for two days. Renting a small apartment off one of those vacation rental sites wasn't cheap. Luckily for me, I had plenty of money stored in overseas banks that weren't in my name, and I didn't have to worry about the International Bureau of Magical Enforcement seizing them.

I've been watching them since I got to town. Trying to get a feel for what they're like. It seems my cousin is mated to a wolf; the thought disgusts me. Even more unusual is that he's part of her pack.

Most supernaturals stick with their own kind; the shifters have packs, the vampires have covens, the faeries have courts, and so on. But their pack went against the norm and opened to include any species of supernaturals.

I had been watching their pack house, the Wimbleton Estate, this morning when I saw the sasquatch leave. I decided to follow him since he was the one I was most interested in.

When he reached the town limits, he found a parking spot in the downtown area, but he had to parallel park. I'm glad I traveled by broom; I hated parallel parking, and that was all the parking available nearby.

On his way down the street, it seemed like everyone he passed stopped to say hi to him, and he happily returned their greeting. It seemed so tedious having to make conversation with so many people, but he didn't seem to mind.

He entered the café and ordered a coffee in a to-go cup and a pastry before taking a seat at a table.

I sat across the room and watched for a little bit, just observing him. As I sat there, I decided he would be my way into his pack. If I was a member of their pack, maybe I could have some protection from the magical enforcement. I couldn't just ask Alexander to let me join his little group. He'd surely send me away, warning everyone to stay away from me. No, it would take more effort on my part. But if I happened to be the mate of the squatch, who they loved, perhaps that would influence them.

With my mind made up, I set to work. I followed one of the café employees to the bathroom, temporarily froze her, and glamoured myself to look like her. Then, I went behind the counter to grab the coffee pot.

When I got there, I took a small vial of the strongest love potion I owned from my magic bag and poured a few drops into the coffee pot when no one was looking.

As I approached the squatch I shooed away the glamour, so I looked like myself again.

"Hi, would you like a top-off?" I asked, gesturing to his cup.

He seemed startled at my voice but quickly straightened and accepted the refill.

"I haven't seen you around here before," he said. "Are you new at the café?"

His cup now had the tainted coffee inside. Now, I just had to wait and hold his attention as he drank it. I needed to be the first person he saw once he took that first sip.

As he drank, I replied, "I just got to town a few days ago. I could really use someone to show me around." I smiled at him and batted my lashes. Yack, I hated playing the bimbo, but it would take a second for the potion to kick in.

It was easy to see when the magic took hold of him. His facial expression went from one of a friendly disposition to a lovesick dopey one.

"I'm happy to help you out."

He could help me all right, help me right into his pack.

ALDER

Earlier That Day

My alarm screamed at me bright and early. My arm, which was numb and tingly from being crunched under my chin, slaps at the annoying device, trying to silence the noise. When my hand connects with the off button, I might have been a little too forceful because it tumbles off the nightstand. Whoops.

I can practically hear my squatch chuckling inside, and I guess I can blame the broken clock on him. Or I could if we weren't the same person. Sometimes, being a sasquatch is a bit confusing. Most types of shifters are in control of both sides of themselves, their humanoid form and their shifted form. Unfortunately, that isn't the case for squatches. We are like two minds shoved into one individual. For the most part, I'm in control of my body.

In my human form, he mostly remains a quiet companion, occasionally sharing his thoughts, though they often seem diluted. Typically, he communicates with grunts and brief commands. However, when I shift forms, he takes control, and I must step back and allow him to guide us. This can be quite frustrating, as he doesn't always listen to me.

"It isn't funny, you brute," I grumble to him. Not that he'll care for my opinions.

Determined not to let this day be ruined, I hop up and get my bed made for the day. That done, I rummage through my closet, looking for the perfect outfit. My options are plaid and more plaid, which are my favorite—shifting those out of the way, I reach into the back, grabbing ahold of a more weather-appropriate option, a black cut-off shirt to pair with my cargo shorts. It's sadly too hot for the plaid.

I creep down the hallway, trying to keep quiet so I don't wake anyone else up. I double-check that I have my supply list for the hardware store, then snag my keys. Since I'll be there running errands, I decide to grab breakfast in town.

The roads are empty on the drive to town, so I arrive sooner than anticipated. The hardware store will not open for another thirty minutes, so I first stop at the cafe for a coffee and a pastry.

They had the raspberry Danish pastries I love so much. I was too excited to eat one and finish it before I even got seated with my coffee. It was delicious, and I wish I had ordered a second one.

Trying to get my mind off the delicacy, I sit back and people-watch as I sip my coffee. It's not often I come to town anymore now that all my closest friends live under the same roof.

The shop is busy this morning, and many people are coming and going, perfect for a distraction. As I watch, I play a little game, human or supernatural. Basically, I make guesses if I think someone is a human or not. I prefer to play this game with a friend. Hadeon is good at it, but he has an unfair advantage. Being a vamp, he's better at sensing other people's species, plus he's pretty old. No one knows for sure how old, but at least a few centuries, compared to the rest of us in our 20s and 30s.

When a woman and little boy walk in, I study them for a minute, human, I think. But the man seated two tables over, he's pretty hair, and my guess is he's a shifter.

It's only a few more minutes until I can leave here and make it to the hardware store at the opening, when I am approached. One of the employees asks if I want a refill of my coffee, which I accept, so I have some coffee to take with me. I'm planning to get out of here shortly, but she starts striking up a conversation. Not wanting to be rude, I humor her.

My squatch has been unhappy from the moment she approached me, grumbling in my mind.

Smells wrong.

What does he mean, smells wrong?

He doesn't specify more, and I sip my coffee. She mentions needing someone to show her around town. I want to mentally say, not my problem, but I hear my mouth volunteering to play tour guide. Huh? Why did I say that? I try to be nice to people, but I have no interest in showing this woman around town. I don't even like being in town all that much, and I don't want to spend time with a random woman. I have my own woman to worry about, one who I'm trying to win over.

It doesn't make any sense why I'm being so agreeable.

I meant to take the coffee cup with me when I left, but I looked down at my hand and realized I had almost finished the whole cup. Strange. Then I looked up at the woman who was still talking to me.

She's a petite waif-like woman with blue hair, short bangs, and black-framed glasses. As I look at her, my heart starts beating frantically in my chest. My hand reached up and clutched my heart.

"What—" I pant through the pain. "What's happening?" I gasp.

She reaches out, rubbing her hand over my mine on my chest. "It's okay, baby. Sometimes, it's overwhelming when you meet your mate for the first time." Her voice croons in my ear, trying to soothe me as I feel like fire is consuming me. This can't be right; it feels so wrong. And I know from the depths of my being that Kai is my mate, not this stranger.

Not long after, I feel an overwhelming euphoria. I'd been missing a vital part of myself, and now it's here—my mate. Yes, my mate. I feel like I'm on cloud nine. But inside my mind, I hear yelling, outrage, and overwhelming sadness. What is that? Deciding it doesn't matter, I ignore it. Nothing can ruin this feeling, this moment.

This small, strange woman climbs into my lap, wrapping her arms around mine in a hug. It's a comforting embrace.

"It's okay," she whispers. "We're together now."

She leaned back, smiling at me, and snapped a few pictures of us snuggled up, one of which showed her kissing my cheek.

"I have to post this!" she exclaims enthusiastically, uploading the pictures of us to her Pack Room app with the caption, 'I can't believe my luck.'

Seven

CELESTE

Two days of being holed up in my rental apartment with the squatch was plenty. Originally, I took him back to my place to make sure the love potion was going to hold up. But I also figured gathering information about him and his friends would be a good idea. I'd prefer to be prepared for any potential threats that might come when we go to the estate.

The squatch proved to be almost utterly useless. Most of the information I got was about his friends. It wasn't anything of importance. Just basic likes and dislikes, relationship dynamics, and drama that developed from everyone living together. There is nothing about pack politics or hierarchy.

I was ready to move forward with my plans. If I was under-prepared for what was to come, I'd just have to wing it. I disliked having to scheme on the fly, but I was quite adept at it.

I didn't have many belongings here since I left almost everything behind when I fled the International Bureau of Magical Enforcement. I shrunk the couple outfits I'd acquired and fit into my magic bag where I housed my spells and ingredients.

"Alright, love, I'm ready for you to take me home," I said in a sickeningly sweet voice. I nuzzled close to Alder's chest. Offering him fake affection in hopes that he believed it and would take me to his community.

A rumbled growl tore out of him before he had a small coughing fit. When he regained his composure, he said, "Sorry, I don't know what that was." Looking sheepish about the whole situation. "I have just the place to take you," he said in excitement.

Deciding it wasn't a good idea to use the same stolen car, I drove to West Virginia; I abandoned it. Then, I found a new car to steal, which was quite easy due to the downtown location.

We made the trip out of town to the Wimbleton estate, but instead of approaching the dark mansion, he directed me to turn. The way we went was hardly a dirt path. I was starting to sweat, thinking maybe the potion wore off and he was playing me, but then my headlights illuminated the shape of a cabin.

"Is this where you live?" I asked.

"No, I've been building this for—." He looked genuinely stumped. "Actually, I don't know why I was building it." He shrugs. "I guess maybe I knew I would meet you, and we'd need it." He smiled and climbed out of the car, so I followed.

He opened the door, which had been unlocked. I don't know what I expected to find here, but it wasn't what I found. There was nothing in here. It was just an empty shell. It had walls, but they weren't painted yet, and there were no finishing touches.

This was going to be a difficult experience, similar to camping, but it would be better than nothing. Being here would also bring me closer to the Fang pack leadership, which was my goal. I would have to make do.

"What am I supposed to sleep on?" I sneered, accidentally breaking character.

Alder didn't seem to notice the slip. He approached and rubbed my arms, trying to soothe me. "You can stay here and relax. I'll head to the storage shed at the main house; there might be an air mattress we can borrow for now."

Before I could refute his idea, he was sprinting out into the night. Great.

About ten minutes later, he was back hauling a deflated air mattress over his shoulder. He looked so proud of himself as he brought it to me. "I found one."

There weren't any lights in here yet, but the electrical outlets worked. He plugged in the mattress, and we switched it on, silently watching as it inflated. It was only a full-size mattress, but it was better than nothing.

"Great, thanks," I said to him as I flopped down in the middle of it. Getting comfortable was no easy feat.

Shortly after I closed my eyes, he cleared his throat, and I opened them to find him hovering over me.

"What?" I replied sharply.

"Are you going to make room for me?"

When my confusion lifted, I couldn't hold back the laughter that built in my chest. "No, I have no plans to sleep next to you."

His face fell, "Where should I sleep?"

"I don't care, just not with me." I turned away, facing the opposite direction.

I heard his heavy steps as he crossed the room. After a minute, I peered over my shoulder to see what he had decided. He lay on the floor, curled in a ball in the corner of the room. That was good. He understood that I was the alpha of this situationship.

Closing my eyes, I took a deep, calming breath and drifted off to sleep.

Eight

KAI

As the pack enforcer, I was expected to be level-headed and fair. Most of the time, I managed to do just that, but ten minutes ago, all of that flew out the window, along with my calm demeanor.

Finley and I had been discussing some protocols she would like to implement for an upcoming trip to another pack's territory. As far as we know, the other pack holds no ill will and intends to have a friendly and productive meeting with us. However, out of an abundance of caution, we still want to be prepared for any situations that may arise. We had just finished talking about the roles we would play when the door to the library room burst open.

Turning toward the door, I braced for trouble, ready to protect my best friend and alpha with all I had. However, I quickly returned to a relaxed posture when I saw it was Callum entering.

He bent forward, his hands resting on his knees, slumping and panting hard. Callum and Finley had hashed out their past and moved on from it, so he was an accepted and valued member of the pack. However, I was still unsure how I felt about the wolf. I wasn't overly concerned about Callum and whatever had brought him here. Finley, who was more worried, jumped out of her chair and approached him.

"Cal, what's going on?" she asked.

Between ragged breaths, he uttered a single word that made my ears perk up: "Alder." Suddenly, I found myself caring about what he had to say.

"What about him?" I demanded, marching forward with determination.

"I went out for a run this morning in my wolf form. When I reached the back of the property near the storage shed, I caught his scent. He has been missing for a few days, so it had to be fresh; I chased it down."

Before I realized what I was doing, I seized him by the collar of his shirt. I pulled him up, bringing us face to face, and then I asked, "And?"

His terrified eyes darted between me and Finley. With a growl, I let go of his collar, making him tumble back to the floor.

He scuttled backward like a crab before speaking again. "Okay, I hate to ruin the surprise, but you would have found out eventually. You guys might know that Alder has been building a cabin in the wooded area. Well, he was building that cabin for you."

Finley, seeming to sense my growing impatience with Callum, stepped between us. To my relief, she took over interrogating her ex. "Okay, focus. Alder's back; that's great, but I'm getting the feeling that there's more to the story. What did you find that got you into the panting mess you showed up here as?"

"I was really worried about Al, so when I followed the trail to the cabin, I didn't bother knocking; I just let myself inside. Upon entering, I immediately saw him, but I was also confused by what I found. He was sleeping with his body curled into a ball in the corner of the room, which was strange enough, but there was someone else there too."

The furrow in his brow was enough to set me on edge. He seemed truly upset about whoever was there. Before we could ask him who it was, the door once again burst open—this time, it was Alexander.

"Let me guess, it was my terrible cousin, Celeste," he said.

How did he know what we were discussing without being present? I loved Finley, so I would accept her mate, but at times he was a nuisance. He constantly interfered in pack matters and used his magic in questionable ways. No one else seemed to notice his intrusion or assumption.

We all turned to Callum for confirmation and saw him nodding his head frantically.

"Yes, she was sleeping on an air mattress." He nervously ran his hands through his hair. Turning back to Xan, he said, "It doesn't make any sense. He's been obsessed with his plans to win Kai over. He thought you'd appreciate having more privacy, so he's been working for months to build this cabin as a grand gesture. So why would he be running around with Celeste and bringing her there? On top of that, something felt very off. I could smell something that was so extremely wrong it unsettled me."

Xan appeared to absorb all the information before he instructed me to wait here and then left the room. This brings me to the present moment, pacing the room, teetering on the edge of losing my composure.

I may oppose the idea of mates, but my most primal instincts are angry about this new turn of events. Moreover, if I'm honest, I'm also very stressed thinking about what might be happening with Alder.

Just as I'm about to disregard Alexander's request for us to wait here, he reenters the room, this time accompanied by Hadeon and Ry.

Once he had explained everything to the newcomers, he declared that we would all go to the cabin to see firsthand what was happening.

We climbed into my SUV while Callum provided directions from the passenger seat.

Early in Alder's cabin construction, I stumbled upon him working shirtless. Since then, I have kept my distance from the area to avoid him. Therefore, I hadn't seen it since it was just a frame. Now, it was truly a sight to behold. While it didn't look fully finished, it was close, at least on the outside.

My heart, which usually had my hard-built walls surrounding it, seemed affected by the knowledge that he had been building this as a home for me. The thought of it now being occupied by another woman made my anger flare. She better not have harmed a hair on my squatch, or it would be her end.

As we climbed the porch, the door opened as if we had been expected. Standing in the doorway was a petite woman with blue hair. She smiled at us before turning her head and yelling, "Babe, your friends are here."

Alder came outside and joined us all on the porch. His lack of greeting was anything but normal. With the golden retriever energy he usually had, he tended to be the friendliest of all of us.

Celeste snuggled into his side, resting her head against his chest, which caused my hackles to rise.

"Now that we're all together, we have some great news to share!" she chirped.

When no one spoke, she continued, "Alder and I would like to formally invite all of you to our mating ceremony."

There were choked gasps and expressions of shock from everyone in our group. I felt as though my ears were ringing from the bombshell she had just dropped. This couldn't be real life.

"It's next week," he said gruffly.

Callum was right; something was terribly wrong.

CELESTE

After informing all of Al's friends about our upcoming mating ceremony, they quickly left. The blonde she-wolf growled low before stomping back to the gothic mansion they all inhabited. One by one, the rest followed. My cousin gave me a very skeptical look before departing. The wolf who found us this morning said he would return shortly to help Alder paint the walls. The vampire lingered the longest but didn't say anything; honestly, it was kind of creepy.

Taking my broom, I flew to town to grab coffee and pastries. Flying always helped my soul feel free and relax me when I was stressed. The wind rushing against my exposed skin was invigorating.

I people-watched while my order was being prepared at the café, but I didn't learn much from the gossip. Most of the people here were human, and I doubted they even knew how many supernaturals lived in their small community.

On the return flight, I had to fly slower and use auto-pilot mode so I could hold onto the coffee tray and the box of pastries. It was less exciting but still quicker than driving.

When I returned to the cabin, I placed the pastries on the counter in the kitchen area. I offered Alder a coffee, and he took a few sips before setting up the supplies for painting.

There was a knock at the door, and I decided it was best to open it. The dark-haired wolf from this morning stood at the threshold. When he said he would return later to help, I hoped he wouldn't keep his word. Unfortunately for me, it seemed he meant what he said. Maybe he would need to have a little accident today to stop him from sniffing around.

Before I could say anything, he slid between me and the door. There wasn't a lot of space, but he somehow managed to avoid making body contact.

"Your wolf friend is here," I said to Alder.

"Callum," the wolf grunted at me.

Whatever, I could care less. I needed Alder to help me connect with the pack for protection, but this wolf was not crucial to my plan. He was more of a nuisance than anything else.

They got busy pouring paint into trays. As the off-white color was being rolled onto the bare walls, Callum glanced at me and said, "Aren't you going to help us?"

Scowling at him before I could mask my expression, I replied, "Manual labor? No, thank you. I'm not good at painting. It would be better for everyone if I just supervised."

He didn't seem thrilled with my answer, but there was no way I was going to get myself covered in paint.

With both of them working on the walls, they made quick progress. It had been a couple of hours since they started, and I realized the squatch hadn't eaten anything yet. Deciding it was best to ensure he was fed, I brought the pastry box over to him. I opened the box in offering, but he tried to take the Danish I had planned to eat. "That one's mine," I said, giving his hand a little swat. I grabbed out a different one and said, "Eat this one." He took it and finished it in two bites, making my lips curl. One was probably fine for now.

As I went to put the box back in the kitchen, I heard footsteps rushing toward me. I turned my head just in time to see Callum stumble. His feet seemed to get caught on each other, causing him to fall forward. The tray of paint in his hands flew in my direction before I could dodge it. The tray must have just been recently refilled because it was full. Almost every drop of that paint landed on me, dripping down my body.

"What the hell!" I yelled at the wolf. A wave of anger, fiercer than anything I had felt in a long time, consumed me.

He looked like he was about to respond, which better be to apologize, but suddenly there was a wheezing noise from behind us. We both turned to look just as Alder hit the floor while clutching at his throat.

Ignoring the river of paint that covered me, I sprinted toward him. What was happening?

Callum and I worked together to roll Alder onto his back. Opening Alder's mouth, he fished a piece of the pastry from inside, which was absolutely disgusting. Even grosser was that Al's tongue was swollen to two times its normal size.

"Why was he eating this?" Callum demanded. He jerked his hand, holding the bite of food in my direction, and saliva flung off, landing on my face. This was more than my stomach could handle, and I started gagging. The whole situation was too gross for me, and I puked, with a little of the vomit landing on my shoes. *Great.*

When I didn't respond to him, he cursed and muttered under his breath about Alder's allergy to the nuts.

"Where is his allergy potion?"

"Why would I know that?" I responded.

"You're supposed to be his mate; you should be aware of his allergies. You should also know where he keeps his remedy potion."

Alder appeared worse for wear as Callum hoisted him over his shoulder and began running toward the main house. It seemed to require significant effort since he was much smaller than the squatch he was trying to carry.

Since he had the situation under control, I would clean myself up before checking on them.

Ten

KAI

"So, all the wolves are in agreement that Alder smelled wrong. Hadeon, do you have any better insight into the smell?" Xan asked.

Wolves possess a keen sense of smell, but vampires, particularly older ones, exhibit even greater abilities than shifters. I was a turbulent mess inside as I waited for him to speak.

"It wasn't something I had smelled before," he replied. Xan rolled his hand in a circular motion, and we all waited for the vamp to continue. "He smelled sweet, but in an overripe, cloying way. The best way I can describe it is as if you forgot about fruit you had in the fridge and it turned rotten, fermenting."

Xan walked over to one of the bookshelves housing his personal grimoire collection and pulled down a couple of books. Only a few volumes remained in his collection since he had to start over after his home and business were burned down by

Fallon, the unhinged alpha whom Finley replaced. Without any further discussion, he began flipping through the delicate pages. He must be quite worried about Alder too, as he wasn't treating his beloved books with the usual care. While he searched, I braced myself for the sound of pages tearing in his haste, but it never came.

He made a hmm sound as he paused on a page, appearing to study it more thoroughly than the others. Just when my hopes began to rise, he said, "No," before resuming his search.

It felt as if little bugs were crawling all over my skin as I sat there waiting. It was agonizing not being able to do anything. The truth was, in this situation, all of us—except for Xan—were utterly useless. There was nothing any of us could do until we understood what was wrong. We all remained silent and let him work.

Callum, who had developed a friendship with Alder, offered to keep an eye on him and Celeste. A couple of hours had passed since he went over to volunteer as a painter. I was starting to worry about how much longer he could keep them distracted and whether we would figure out Alder's malady when there was a loud BANG from the front of the house. Instantly, we were on our feet and sprinting from the room. My wolf instincts told me that something was seriously wrong.

We had just reached the entry area when a sweaty Callum came into view. He was bent over, barely able to stagger forward with a limp Alder on his back.

Heart racing, I threw myself toward them. I ducked under one of Al's arms and helped support some of his weight.

Hadeon grabbed the other side, enabling Callum to free himself from his hunched position.

He slumped onto the floor, panting, before Finley helped him up. We all hurried to Xan's workroom, where we laid Al on a table for examination.

Seeing his lips had a slightly blue tinge sent panic spiraling within me. I could see Callum's mouth forming words, but I couldn't hear anything over the sound of my erratic heartbeat.

Whatever Callum said to Xan got him moving. He crossed the room and began rummaging through his supplies before returning to the prone body of our friend.

Finley must have sensed how affected I was, for she came over and wrapped her arm around me. My eyes pricked with pain, and it took a couple of minutes before I realized I was crying. I didn't notice the tears sliding down my cheeks until Finley wiped them away.

I've done nothing but treat Alder poorly and avoid him since I discovered he was my mate. But now, faced with the possibility of losing him, all I can do is beg the fates for another chance. I silently plead for him to be okay and for a chance to improve the relationship between us.

The room was deathly silent as Xan poured a vial of liquid into Alder's mouth. We collectively held our breath, waiting for something, anything, to happen—a sign that everything would be okay.

When it felt as if my world was about to crumble, a gasp erupted from the table. Alder shot up into a sitting position and began to cough violently.

"Welcome back," Xan said, giving him a friendly pat on the back.

"Back?" he whispered.

"You experienced a severe allergic reaction. You stopped breathing for a minute. We managed to get you help just in time. Callum saved your life."

My eyes turned to appraise the wolf with newfound respect. I had always disliked Callum because of his past with Finley, even after they hashed it out, but I would no longer hold it against him. Going forward, he would be someone of great value to me. He is the reason my mate is alive.

Yes, my mate. It was time to acknowledge and accept what Alder is to me. *Mine*.

XAN

"Drink this," I said as I handed over a small vial.

Al sniffed it, which was a bad idea. The potion smelled foul and tasted even worse—at least, that's what I've been told, probably because the main ingredient was fermented frog intestines. Maybe I should warn him after all. Nah, we'll just roll with it. If he knew about it, he'd fight harder against taking it. "What is it?" Al narrowed his eyes suspiciously.

Hadeon, who was standing next to Al, pointed across the room and asked again, "What's that?" When Al turned to look, Hadeon took advantage of his vampiric speed and poured the contents of the vial into his mouth before Al could protest. It might have been an underhanded trick, but it was for the best. Some sputtering and hacking indicated that the liquid was swallowed, and it didn't take long for the effects to kick in.

He released a terrifying roar before his trembling body fell from the table. He landed on the floor before losing the battle with the potion and transforming into his squatch form. Again, the thought crossed my mind that maybe I should have warned him, but it's a bit late now. Ah, oh well. The allergy mix I gave him helped bring him back from the severe reaction he had, but to fully heal in a timely manner, it was necessary for him to change forms. It would have been difficult for him to change without assistance in his current state.

Alder sprung up quickly from the floor and seemed agitated. He paced back and forth for a minute before seeming to settle down. It was in our best interest for him to remain calm since he was over seven feet tall in squatch form and had immense strength. It was paramount not to get into a fight with him; we'd most likely lose.

Alder climbed onto the table once again, and I was surprised that the poor thing didn't collapse under the weight of his larger form. Kai, who had been standing near him as he paced, moved closer to the table, her body braced almost as if she were ready to leap into the fray if anything crazy happened. It made me chuckle a little to watch. For someone who wanted nothing to do with mates or my squatch friend, she sure was protective of him. I had no doubt that eventually they would figure things out and be together.

When the door to the room opened, my mind wandered away, and I wondered what the future might hold. It was Callum; I'd sent him to get some water for everyone. Consuming a good amount of water over the next few days would be especially important for Alder, who would need to flush toxins from his system.

He poured one of the water bottles into a large bowl, trying to make it easier for Alder to hold with his ginormous squatch hands. Then he turned and started approaching Al and Kai. Before he could get close, a low, deep growl emerged, and Alder sprang forward. I braced myself, thinking he was triggered and going to attack. Instead, he wrapped his arm around Kai and pulled her onto his lap, trapping her with his arms.

Kai looked genuinely angry at the possessive move. Callum merely laughed.

With hands raised in a placating gesture, he approached. "Don't worry, big guy; we all know she's yours."

Alder's lip curled back into a snarl, revealing fangs larger than my pointer finger, but he didn't growl again. Callum cautiously approached and held out the water in offering.

After he accepted the bowl of water, we all settled in to wait for a bit. It would be a couple of hours before the potion that forced his change wore off. We all took seats and relaxed, but despite the calm atmosphere, Alder still didn't release his hold on Kai.

I'd need to examine him again, but he looked much better when he reverted to human form. Just as I was about to start, the door was thrown open with such force that it hit the wall with a thud. In sprinted my wayward cousin.

Celeste rushed straight to Alder, acting completely panicked over his condition, even though she hadn't come earlier when he was near death. I hoped I wasn't the only one who could see through her superficial behavior.

Alder saw her, and there was undoubtedly some kind of magic at work. His eyes seemed almost glazed over as he carelessly tossed Kai aside before rushing to Celeste.

Anger simmered within me upon witnessing it. I had no doubt that my cousin had manipulated his mind in some way, and I was determined to uncover the truth.

Twelve

KAI

This week has dragged painfully slowly. Alder has made a full recovery from his allergic reaction and has reverted to the oddly blank version of himself that he's been since Celeste came into the picture. It took a few days of collaboration between Hadeon and Xan, but they figured out what was wrong. We shifters first noticed that his scent was off. With Hadeon's superior vampire sense of smell, he was able to describe it in detail to Xan, who spent days researching and contacting other witches and warlocks to identify the magic used.

It turns out he's under a powerful love potion- one so strong that few methods exist to free the affected person from its thrall. The only option we have to break the spell on Alder is for him to be claimed by his fate's blessed mate. All other options would take too long to create a counteractive potion, which wouldn't be ready in time to interrupt the mating ceremony between him and Celeste.

Since the discovery of the love potion, Callum has been tasked with watching over them. He was chosen for this duty because he appears non-threatening and had previously worked at the cabin. Ever since, he's been a thorn in Celeste's side, hardly allowing them any alone time.

Today is the mating ceremony, which will take place deep in the Monongahela National Forest. We are all pretending to be going along with this farce so we can stop it.

We drove to the parking lot designated for the hiking trail and met there. We were all dressed in hiking attire and packed a bag of dressy clothes to change into when we got there, as we needed to look like happy attendees.

Unintentionally, I slammed the driver's door of my SUV as I got out. The stress of what I had to do today was overwhelming me with emotions. When I was young, I witnessed the destruction that having a partner can bring, so I swore I would never have one. Growing up, my parents were completely awful to each other but claimed to love one another. There may not have been physical violence between them, but they were toxic together, constantly manipulating one another and creating an emotionally destructive environment, even to the detriment of my well-being.

Today, I will break the vow I made all those years ago and claim my mate to free him from Celeste's control. The good thing for me is that I've gotten to know Alder, and he's a cinnamon roll in human form. He doesn't have an aggressive bone in his body. I once looked down on him for his perspective, but now I'm thankful for his laid-back, friendly demeanor. I'd never admit it out loud, but maybe being with him would be a good thing; perhaps I could finally lower the walls around my heart. I've spent too long keeping everyone out, sometimes even my best friend.

"Alder in the woods? This must have been Celeste's idea," a disgruntled Xan stated. He opened the trunk of his vehicle and pulled out the mesh netting that Alder usually wears in the woods because of his numerous allergies. "I bet Celeste doesn't even realize he shouldn't be out here, and if she did know, I guarantee she wouldn't care. His safety is the least of her concerns. Fortunately, I brought his allergy potions with me just in case."

Geared up, we started the trek to the location we were sent to. Hadeon, being the best at logistics and planning, already mapped out the path. The forest is beautiful, but the longer we walk, the angrier I get. Who invites people to such an important event and then expects them to put in so much effort just to get there?

It takes an hour and a half to reach our destination. A few minutes away, we stop to change into our formal wear. I'm grateful that Finley packed some wipes in her bag, so I grab a few to wipe away some of the sweat from my body.

Once we are dressed in our fancy clothes, we complete the walk, which is thankfully not too strenuous.

We enter a clearing, and I silently take it all in for a minute. Small fairy lights are strung between the treetops. A few overturned logs have been covered with a lace runner, appearing to be seating for this event. An arch is set up to one side of the clearing, with live plants woven through the wooden slats. How did she even get all of this stuff out here?

Celeste sees us and approaches to greet us.

"You made it!" she exclaims with excitement. I reluctantly admit she looks very pretty tonight. Her floor-length silk dress is white at the straps and transforms into a deep blue at the end. It perfectly matches her midnight blue hair, which has flowers woven into it.

Alexander steps up to greet his cousin, taking one for the team. "Wouldn't miss it for the world," he says in a voice so charming that it's almost believable—if I didn't know the truth.

They embrace, and everyone else showers her with greetings and compliments. I tune them out, though. My mind is set on one thing right now. I search around us for Alder and can't seem to find him anywhere. Irritation spikes under my skin, feeling like thorns against my flesh. This wasn't what we planned. They were supposed to distract her, and I was to sneak away to Alder. But he isn't here, which ruins our plan.

Seeming to notice the missing squatch, I hear Callum ask the question we are all wondering: "Where's Al?"

She offers a slight smile, something inscrutable shining behind her eyes as she assures us that he will be here soon.

Where is he? Did she do something to him?

She instructs everyone to take a seat, and we do. Our plan isn't going as planned, and now we'll have to pivot. Once we are all sitting on the logs, she whistles loudly. Immediately after, a large shadow falls from the sky.

With a thump, the figure lands in a crouch. Only then do we realize it's Alder; he must have been up in the trees somewhere. What was he doing up there?

Standing under the decorative arch, Celeste links hands with him. They stare into each other's eyes when Hadeon looks at me. I understand the meaning; it's go time.

With the supernatural speed of his kind, he is a blur of motion as he tackles Celeste and holds her hostage until this is over. I start sprinting forward the moment he gives the signal, and within seconds, I am standing in front of Alder. He looks at me with a confused expression but shows no other recognition. I grab his wrist and lift it up. Shifting my teeth from human to wolf, I quickly bite deep into his flesh. The slight metallic tang reaches my taste buds before I disengage my bite. It isn't as off-putting as I imagined; I wonder if it's like that for Hadeon and other vamps, or if it's even better.

I drop Alder's arm just as he releases a roar and suddenly shifts into his squatch form. His natural form is intimidatingly large. With forest green eyes locked on mine, he begins stalking toward me with predatory intent. For every step he takes toward me, I take two steps back, yet he keeps coming.

When he closes the distance between us, my composure vanishes, and my eyes widen in fear. Did it work? He seems a bit angry. Is he going to attack?

Suddenly, I'm yanked forward, colliding with his solid frame. With snake-like speed, he strikes, his teeth sinking into my shoulder.

Thirteen

ALDER

My teeth unclench from a shoulder, and the realization that something weird is happening jolts me from a fog. I look around, trying to figure out what the hell is happening. When I pull back, I see the blood dripping from the fresh bite, and instinct takes over as I lean in and lick the wound, sealing the mark in the delectable flesh.

Standing at full height, I see Kai's sapphire eyes glowing in the dim light. Her expression appears unreadable, but her eyes give her away, feelings swirling in their dark cerulean depths. The bond that joins our souls betrays her as well. Despite her calm exterior, I can feel so many emotions from her, the heaviest of which are fear and uncertainty, all tinged with a bit of excitement.

The fear feels unsettling coming from such a strong and assured woman like Kai. Is her fear directed towards me? Fates, I can only pray it isn't. I would never do anything to hurt her; just the thought of it kills me.

We stare at each other for a minute while chaos explodes all around us, yet I can't bring myself to look away. The realization that we have just created a mating bond elates me like nothing else ever could. This is something I have longed for but never expected to happen.

Screaming jolts me from my reverie.

"You ruined it!" A female voice I don't recognize yells at the top of her lungs. "This is all your fault!" She points an accusing finger in Kai's direction as she tries, and fails, to run our way. Hadeon holds her back as she struggles.

I can feel my brows furrow in confusion. Who is she? Regardless of who she is, she seems very angry at Kai, and I'm unsure why. However, she won't continue to use that tone with my mate. A growl I didn't know I could produce escapes me as I step in front of Kai, shielding her from the screeching banshee.

Callum looks at me with wide eyes, then grins and gives me a thumbs-up. I'm so confused fucking, but I go along with it since it feels right.

When the woman stops struggling, Hadeon releases her, and with her no longer restrained, she falls to the ground. She remains there, panting as she tries to regain control of her breathing after her outburst.

Xan, standing near the edge of the clearing, stalks to my side. He gives a cutting glare at the stranger before addressing her.

"Why did you spell' Alder'?" he demands.

Spell me, what the fuck is he talking about?

She grins at him, and it's a terrifying sight to behold. There is nothing but malice in her expression as she does so.

"I needed the pack's protection, and I thought mating with your Neanderthal friend would help," she says, completely unrepentant.

My chest pangs a little at the statement, though. Ouch. Not only did she compare me to a cave person, she was also trying to use me. But I think the worst part is realizing that whatever scheme this person concocted is the only reason my mate accepted me. Kai has never wanted to be with me, and now we are stuck together for all eternity. It hurts knowing she didn't choose me. The thought makes my heart feel like it's crumbling. The urge to run is strong.

Before I can act on the impulses I'm feeling, Xan approaches me and pulls out some items from his bag. He hands me a vial and a rolled-up netting. Sniffing the vial, I realize it's the potion he brews for my allergies. The net is something I usually wear when I need to go into the woods to protect myself from the insects that I'm allergic to.

"I believed it was wiser to be safe than sorry," he says, gesturing for me to drink the potion.

I mechanically accept the items and follow the instructions. I pop the vial's lid and down its contents in a single gulp, then I put on the net suit, draping it over my body.

Normally, none of this would phase me; I'm used to taking these precautions. But at the moment, I feel nothing but sheer embarrassment over it, probably because I already feel the self-consciousness of being unwanted.

My friends continue for a while, questioning the stranger, whose name I learn is Celeste. She's apparently Xan's evil cousin and a fugitive currently wanted by the International Bureau of Magical Enforcement. That's how we got roped into her scheming.

She intended to use the love spell on me, deceiving me into becoming her chosen mate, while relying on the pack to safeguard her from the consequences of her illegal lifestyle.

The next steps are being discussed. When Finley suggests they call the Bureau and turn her over to them, something happens. Suddenly, there is a type of magical explosion. Smoke fills the clearing until we can't see anything, and everyone coughs from breathing it in.

Xan chants strangely, and within a few minutes, the area is clear again—except when we look around, Celeste is gone.

Finley scoffs in irritation, but Knox's reaction surprises everyone. He is in a blind panic. He sprints into the tree line, yelling that she is his mate, and that he needs to go with her.

We all looked at each other in stunned silence. When it became clear that he wasn't coming back, we all started to pack up and hike back to the cars.

Kai and I are given some space. We need to clarify a few matters and discuss them further.

We linger a short distance behind the group as we walk. She's still wearing the emerald silk dress from the ceremony. The moonlight caressing her skin and pale hair creates a stunning sight. I don't think she's ever looked more beautiful.

Clearing my throat, my heart skips a beat as I bring voice to the promise, I can give her.

"We may not be immortal, but I will spend however long it takes to make you happy. Even if it takes most of our lives, I'll prove myself to you. I'll love you every day until you recognize that we are inevitable. Someday you will no longer regret me," I whisper the declaration as it is swallowed up by the night air.

Fourteen

ALDER

We had a quiet and very awkward drive back to the estate. Everyone else was trying to be nice and give Kai and me some alone time, but in the silence of this ride, I wished they hadn't. It would be great to have someone around to help break the thick tension in the air.

When we arrive back at the old Victorian house that we both call home, we get out of Kai's SUV without a word. Thankfully, everyone else arrives just after us.

"I'm glad you're back to being yourself," Callum says as he throws his arm over my shoulder.

"Yeah, me too," I say, swallowing hard. I can't recall anything that's happened recently. It's utterly unnerving.

Once we are all in the library—where we usually hold our meetings—Ry goes straight to the bar cart. He and his friend, Leora, hand out tumblers to everyone, and then Hadeon follows behind them, pouring a few fingers' worth of whiskey into each glass.

"I can add a touch of magic to the whiskey if anyone desires a mood lift," Leora offers. She's a light fairy and, when needed, can perform wondrous feats to brighten a sour mood.

"Too soon," I whisper.

"I believe we've encountered enough magical interference for now," Xan states, which surprises me. As a warlock, he's always eager to use magic. It seems that my recent incident has impacted my best friend.

I toss the alcohol back, savoring the burn, and extend the glass for Hadeon to refill. He obliges without comment.

Once everyone has started drinking, I ask, "Now, who would like to tell me what on earth has been happening?"

In true alpha fashion, Finley informs me about the time I'm missing from my memory.

"We knew something was wrong," Kai says. It just took us a little bit to figure it out. I just knew it didn't make sense."

"Hadeon was a great help in discovering the love potion. His vampire senses helped identify a scent we couldn't pinpoint," Xan praises.

"Celeste made a run for it, so we don't have to worry about her any longer—at least for a little while. But she shouldn't get away with this," Kai nearly growls. My inner squatch sits up inside me, puffing his chest at our mate's reaction to someone trying to harm us. Smug asshole. Not that I'm much better.

Everyone is busy expressing their agreement with her as my cell phone rings. It's a blocked number, and at first, I hesitate, feeling too nervous to answer in case it's Celeste.

With the group's encouragement, I finally answered and chose to put it on speaker.

"Hello?"

"Hello, am I speaking with Alder Waldvogel?" a gruff voice asks.

"Um, yes. Who is this?" My tone relaxes more once I realize it isn't Celeste on the other end of the line.

"This is Agent Schaffer with the International Bureau of Magical Enforcement. My partner and I have been searching for a wanted witch named Celeste Blackmore. We have learned that you may have had recent interactions with her. We would like to meet with you to ask a few questions."

When I scan the room, everyone gazes back at me with wide eyes.

"Yes, you could say that I have seen her."

"Would you be able to meet with my partner, Agent Laramie, and me tomorrow?" he asks.

"I would meet with you; unfortunately, Celeste used a spell on me. I've recently been released from the magic, but I don't really remember anything from the last few weeks."

Kai scowls at me and jabs me in the gut with her elbow.

At her fierce look, I continue, "However, if you're fine with me bringing a few of my pack members to the meeting, they could help answer any questions you have."

When Agent Schaffer agrees to our having additional company at the meeting, we finalize plans, and I end the call.

"Oh, this will be so much fun," Xan cackles with an evil gleam in his eyes.

Fifteen

ALDER

Last night, instead of returning to the cabin, I stayed in my old room in the packhouse. I've scheduled a specialized cleaner to come and freshen up the cabin, so it won't smell like Celeste anymore. My squatch was very unsettled by the remnants of her scent there. It was a fitful night of sleep, knowing my mate was under the same roof but not with me.

The meeting with the agents will take place shortly. We agreed to meet at Milson's, a small diner about an hour away from our pack house.

I'd never been before, but many of the residents of Silver Ridge talk about it frequently. It's a bit of a drive, but supposedly, they have the best breakfast spread in a four-county area—something I hope to be true.

We may be gathering there to make a statement about Celeste to the agents, but that doesn't mean I won't take the opportunity to enjoy some amazing breakfast food while we're there.

I looked up the place online, and I've already decided on ordering what was described as the 'Virginian.' It was the largest breakfast combo, featuring eggs, hashbrowns, toast, waffles, ham, bacon, and sausage. A meal that includes three types of meat? Count me in for that!

Ultimately, Ry and Leora stayed home while the rest of us went to the meeting.

Since Kai has an SUV with third-row seating, she volunteered to drive. Hadeon tried his best to convince her to let him drive—the vamp has a few control issues—but ultimately was turned down.

We arrive at the dinner with exactly two minutes to spare. Kai parallel parks the SUV like a pro, which is a total turn-on to see her confidently maneuver this large vehicle.

We're walking up to the diner when I suddenly see Hadeon holding the door open. That stinking vampire speed- I didn't even see him move. While I know that his speed can be handy, sometimes I can't help but feel a little perturbed when he uses it so needlessly. Okay, so it's probably just a hint of jealousy showing. Being a squatch—quite literally one of the largest humanoid types of supernatural species—doesn't exactly come with the added abilities of speed or agility.

As I approach the door, I choose to overlook his annoying habit when I catch a whiff of the food wafting through the open entryway.

My squatch is doing the equivalent of a happy, wiggly dance in my mind at the thought of food.

When we enter, I see a middle-aged bald man wave us in his direction. Seeing the apparel he and his tablemate are wearing, it's easy to see that these must be agents Schaffer and Laramie. As we head toward the duo, I realize it's a little weird that he knows who we are.

On the phone, I didn't specify how many of us from our pack would attend the meeting, but the table they chose has enough space to accommodate all of us.

The middle-aged man stands and introduces himself as Agent Schaffer and his partner as Laramie. We follow suit with introductions and then take a seat at the table.

Schaffer steeples his hands in front of him as he watches me. However, he doesn't begin talking or asking questions, and neither does Laramie, so the atmosphere becomes awkward quickly.

Before the strangeness can continue for long, an older woman introduces herself as our waitress, Glenda, and takes our order. At first, Kai said she wasn't going to order anything, but after a low growl from me, she ended up requesting bacon and eggs. I want to say, "that's my good girl, " but knowing she isn't ready for that, I keep it to myself. It's only after Glenda departs that Schaffer speaks.

"So, we received information that Celeste was spotted in the area and may have had contact with you, Mr. Waldvogel. Based on our conversation last night, I assume this is accurate?" he asks.

"Yes, sir."

"And how did you come to be in contact with the wanted witch?" Laramie asks.

"I brought her to our pack territory. At the time, it wasn't known that she had used a very potent love potion on me, and she convinced me to bring her there," I confess. I know it isn't something I could have controlled due to being spelled, but I feel very guilty about bringing her to our pack house. From everything I've learned about her after her departure, she's extremely dangerous. I wouldn't have been able to live with the guilt if something bad had happened to any of the people I care about.

"How did you discover that you were under her magical control?" Schaffer asks.

I allow Xan to explain this since I don't know the specifics and Xan was highly involved in helping figure it out. As I listen to them, I start eating. Fates, the rumors about the food were true. It's probably one of the best breakfasts I've ever had.

They ask a series of follow-up questions, which are answered by either Xan or Hadeon.

Once the agents are satisfied with their list of questions, they share some details about the case with us. Celeste is wanted for numerous criminal offenses related to the use of banned magic, most of which have caused harm to humans and other supernatural beings, including bodily harm and even death.

We explained that she fled after the failed bonding attempt and that Knox pursued her. Callum made sure to communicate that his brother was not involved in any of the trouble caused by Celeste but was convinced she was his mate, so he chased after her. The poor guy got a bit flustered trying to convince them that his brother wasn't a troublemaker and wouldn't assist Celeste with her criminal activities. I hope what he said is true, but if a mate bond is genuinely at play, it could influence his desire to help her.

After close to an hour, the agents gathered everything they needed from us and excused themselves. They left us with both their business cards and expressed their concern that this might not be the last we see of Celeste. They believe it's possible she will return to our pack territory and seek revenge for us ruining her plans. Apparently, she's rumored to be a very prideful witch and likely won't allow the blow to her ego to go unanswered. After hearing all the horrible crimes she's committed, I truly hope they're wrong and that we don't get a repeat visit from her.

Sixteen

KAI

Against all protests, I've been sequestered to the backseat, leaving me sitting closer than I'd prefer to Alder—the gentle sasquatch, my mate. Gah, *my mate*. I'm still having a hard time processing that.

It's been a few days since we met with the agents about Celeste, but I've been swiftly avoiding him by diving into work. I was hoping to evade the moment of defining the relationship that I knew would come. Technically, we're now mated and were fated, but I never planned for any of this. If things hadn't happened to practically force my hand, I don't know if I would have ever accepted our bond.

The car ride has been awkward since we left the pack house thirty minutes ago, but we have a six-hour drive to look forward to. This trip has been in the works for several weeks, and despite our recent troubles, this is an important appointment.

The territory we are heading to is located in Kentucky, midway between Lexington and Louisville. It belongs to the Harrison pack. They invited us to discuss our experience integrating non-wolf shifters into our pack. The alpha of Harrison hopes to persuade his council that successful integration is possible. This would enhance stability in their area and improve interspecies relations.

Next to me, Alder shifted slightly, but due to his size, his side brushed against my shoulder and thigh. I took what should have been a fortifying breath, but sitting so close to him caused his scent to invade my nose. It frustrates me irrationally that he smells so incredibly good, like a forest in autumn.

Clearing my throat, I search for a distraction from both my reaction to him and the possibility of anyone else noticing it.

"Tell me what you know about the Harrison pack," I say to no one in particular.

From the front passenger seat, Finley replies, "Their alpha is Riggs Harrison. He has overseen the Harrison pack for the last two years. It was very controversial when he assumed the alpha position because the pack had never had an alpha that young; he was only twenty at the time. He has had to defend his position against challenges so often that they hold an open challenge period once a month."

"I imagine that if he has already struggled with respect in his position because of his age, there may be some packmates who will be unhappy if he chooses to open the pack to supernaturals outside the wolf community. We haven't received much pushback, but not everyone is as open-minded as we are," I point out.

"You're on the right track with that thinking," she confirms. "They structure their pack a bit differently than we do. They have a council that votes on major decisions for the pack. They typically support the alpha's proposals, but this process helps the entire pack feel more secure about the outcomes. They don't want to feel as though they're entrusting their pack's fate to a child—not my words," she rolls her eyes. "That's why we'll be meeting with the council while we're there as well."

"What do we know about the council?" Xan asks from the driver's seat.

"There are five members of the council. When it was created, only five original families founded the pack. Each family has a representative who holds a seat on the council."

"What about the Harrison family's seat? I assume it's not Riggs since he's the alpha," I ask her. The alpha comes from a founding family, so I'm curious to know who occupies Harrison's council seat.

"A cousin from the Harrison family occupies the seat. He's in his sixties and is considered the elder of the family," she responds.

When no one asks any more questions, we sit in silence as we drive. I ponder the fact that Riggs is the alpha. It's curious to me that the elder of the Harrison family wouldn't be in charge. Who held the alpha position before Riggs? How did the transfer of power occur?

There are some things we won't know about the pack since we aren't part of it. As Fang's second-in-command and enforcer, ensuring our alpha's safety on this trip is my responsibility. It's my job to be as knowledgeable as I can about the people we will meet and the places we will go.

Fortunately, I still have a cellular signal, so I take out my phone to conduct some additional research.

Seventeen

ALDER

The scenery changed drastically as we approached the Harrison Pack land. It went from empty fields and farms to a town that sprung from nothing.

When we drove through the main strip of town, it was easy to spot a combination of humans and supernatural beings.

The small, family-owned shops and boutiques had a charming appeal to them.

Just a few minutes outside the town, we approached what would look to anyone else like a gated community—this was the pack land.

From what I'd read, they owned over 600 acres of land. Their primary residence was surrounded by a tall black wrought-iron fence with a guard house stationed at the entrance.

Xan stopped at the gate and rolled down his window to speak with the guard.

"Name?" the stout man in uniform asked.

"Alexander Moretti. These are some of my packmates. We have an appointment with Alpha Harrison," he replied in a no-nonsense tone. I believe it was one of the first times I had ever known Xan to sound so business-like, rather than the agent of chaos he typically presents as.

The guard glanced at the screen on his tablet briefly before confirming that he had us listed. He then asked us to wait a moment and ducked back into the small building.

When he returned, he held four badges on bright orange lanyards.

"These are your visitor passes. We kindly ask that you wear these throughout your visit, and we will collect them upon your departure."

Once we wore the badges, he gave us directions and allowed us to enter.

Xan followed the gravel drive that veered left through wooded land. Once we reached a clearing, the main house came into view. "House" was the wrong name for the place—it was a fate's damn mansion.

Fang was the largest shifter pack in North America, but none of the properties that have housed the alphas, current or past, has ever been this immense. This made me question how the pack earned its money.

We were greeted by several men who were similar in height to the wolf shifters from our pack. They were polite but didn't seem overly enthusiastic about seeing us, which made me wonder how the meeting would go.

One of the three stepped forward, introduced himself as Kade, and beckoned us to follow him to meet the alpha.

When we entered the mansion, Xan let out a low whistle and gazed at me with wide eyes. I could sense he was pondering the same question I had when we arrived: "How?"

The group quietly guided us through the house, where we ascended to the second floor and walked down a long hallway. The estate was vast, but it felt almost eerie in its emptiness. We hadn't encountered a single person since we entered.

When we reached a red, intricately carved door, Kade knocked firmly against the wood. When the voice inside said to enter, we were let into the room, but the men who led us there didn't stay.

The room appeared to be some sort of parlor. It was large and adorned with antique velvet couches. The table between them was made of deep chocolate-colored wood, featuring carvings of flowers. I felt uncomfortably out of place amidst our gilded surroundings. My squatch echoed this sentiment with a *har-rumph*.

A man in a full suit, that looked freshly pressed and had his hair slicked back, stood from one of the couches before setting a tumbler of golden liquid on a coaster.

"Ah, you must be from Fang," he said. Smiling at us, he approached and introduced himself as Riggs.

Finley stepped forward and shook his proffered hand. "Nice to meet you; I'm Finley, the alpha of Fang." Gesturing to Xan, she continued, "This is my mate, Alexander."

He looked between them with interest. "I've heard so much about both of you. You're truly breaking the norm among the supernatural—being a female alpha and choosing a warlock as your mate."

I heard a low growl from Kai, who was still standing closer to me than the group. Looking at her, I silently conveyed, 'You good?'

"He is my fate's blessed mate," Finley corrected firmly. The expression on her face spoke volumes. She wouldn't tolerate any nonsense if this wolf tried to convince her that she should have chosen a wolf over Xan.

With his hands raised in a placating gesture, he replied, "I apologize if that seemed rude; that was never my intention. I just find it fascinating."

Seemingly momentarily assuaged, he extended a hand toward Kai and me. "And who have you brought with you today?"

Kai stepped forward, but I noticed she didn't shake his hand. She gave him a penetrating look that I felt could sear his soul and introduced us, "I'm Kai, Finley's second in command and enforcer. And this is my mate, Alder," she extended her hand toward me as if showing off a prize won on a game show. As he looked me up and down, as if assessing me, Kai added, "A sasquatch."

Riggs seemed to jolt slightly at the suddenly revealed fact. I'm not sure if anyone else noticed the movement because it was so subtle, but I certainly saw it before he quickly masked his surprise.

"How interesting," was the only reply we received from him. However, the tone in which he said it did not suggest he found it interesting; instead, it seemed more like he was disgusted. He did not offer to shake my hand, and he kept a wary eye on me.

From his reaction, I wondered if he had something against sasquatches or if it was just me in particular that he wasn't fond of. We were here today to talk about interspecies integration into wolf packs. If he was disturbed by the alpha mating a warlock and her enforcer mating a squatch, I wasn't sure how productive this meeting would truly be. If he felt wolves were superior to other supernaturals, this wouldn't work at all.

Just as the silence in the room began to feel uncomfortable, a knock at the door broke the stillness.

When the alpha permitted the knocker to enter, Kade poked his head into the room. He gave a slight bow before addressing the alpha, "Sir, the council is ready to start." Then, he excused himself.

Riggs cleared his throat and said, "Well, let's get this show on the road, shall we?"

We followed him from the room to the meeting, and as we walked, I kept wondering what we were getting ourselves into.

Eighteen

KAI

We left the meeting room with frustration trailing behind us. We spoke with the Harrison pack council for hours, and it felt like they just kept repeating themselves. The whole point of coming here was that they were supposedly ready and willing to incorporate other species into their pack. However, judging by how the conversation went, it was clear that couldn't be further from the truth. The only person who seemed eager to add new members to their group was the alpha, but we already knew that the council held significant sway in decision-making. The meeting was fruitless and likely a huge waste of everyone's time.

Riggs walked ahead of the four of us from Fang, leading the way back to the main section of the house. A grunt of irritation escaped Xan as the council headed down the hallway in the opposite direction. To my surprise, he seemed to be the most affected by the failed meeting. I wondered if it was because, as a former outsider to our pack, he understood what the success of other packs' integration would entail. He emerged from the room moodier than usual.

When we arrived back at the alpha's office, he invited us in before shutting the door.

"Well, that could have gone better," he stated, clearly aware of the situation, with his head hung low.

"That was a disaster," Xan replied as he flopped onto the small couch. He crossed his arms and stared blankly at the ceiling; clearly, he had activated his pouting mode.

"I know it was rough, but I believe that if I continue working with the council, they will eventually agree. I just need to demonstrate how beneficial this could be for the pack. I should show them the positives, so to speak." Riggs looked thoughtful for a moment, as if he were mentally making a pro-con list. "Nevertheless, I appreciate you coming all this way to speak with us."

"It was our pleasure," Finley said diplomatically. Sometimes it was amusing to see her in the alpha role; if she weren't alpha, I almost thought she would share her true thoughts on the situation rather than be polite. Some comments made by the council members were increasingly prejudiced. I remember one remark from an older man, who said that wolves shouldn't lower their status by intermingling with inferior bloodlines. I could tolerate a lot, but that remark made my hackles rise. In response, my wolf released a fierce growl, which silenced him.

Neither Finley nor I intended to create offspring with our mates at this time, but if we ever did, it would be no one else's business. Just thinking about having a child be bullied for not being "wolf enough" had me envisioning tearing apart the flesh of the perpetrator. The bloody musings lifted my spirits immensely.

When Finley shot me a curious glance because of the smirk I had, I merely shrugged. Perhaps I could explain later if she raises the topic. She would wholeheartedly support my violent plans against anyone who threatened our future kids.

Oh fates. I didn't even know if I wanted to be mated; it certainly was never something I planned. I didn't need to think about our hypothetical future.

As Finley's second, it was my job to be here, so I refocused on the discussion.

"We planned to leave a few hours ago, but since our departure was delayed, could you let me know if there is a hotel nearby? We'll likely find a local place to stay the night, so we'll be well-rested for our drive back tomorrow."

Xan and Alder didn't object to her decision to find a place for the night, but the change of plans made me uncomfortable. Finley was my best friend, so of course, I wouldn't want anything to happen to her, but it was literally my job now to keep her safe. A change in plans means that all my carefully planned security measures went out the window. I'd have to do some research on wherever we ended up getting rooms.

Riggs waved her off. "Nonsense. You will do no such thing." Shaking his head, he continued, "It is our fault you were delayed. Allow us to make up for it. We have plenty of space here in the alpha household. I'll have a staff member prepare some rooms; I insist you stay here."

My hopes of leaving this place behind were dashed when Finley accepted the offer.

"Wonderful," he exclaimed. "Since you'll be here, I'd like to extend an invitation for all of you to attend our monthly gathering. If you feel too tired, please feel free to skip it, but I thought you might enjoy mingling with some of the pack. I sense that the council has given you the impression that we're all pompous imbeciles, and I'd appreciate the opportunity to set the record straight." He grimaced slightly at that, but he wasn't wrong.

The alpha may lead a group with some seriously bigoted elders, but you couldn't say he was inefficient. Within a couple of minutes of his extending an offer for us to stay the night, a staff member arrived to show us to our assigned rooms.

We followed the woman as she led us through the mansion. I was focused on keeping track of the hallways, exits, and potential safety hazards when our group suddenly stopped.

"These are the two rooms that the alpha had me prepare," she gestured toward the side-by-side doors.

Two rooms for the four of us, *oh fates.*

Nineteen

KAI

After we changed into appropriate clothing, we were led through the backyard to a wooded trail. Full darkness had set in, making the flashlights we received a necessity—well, for everyone except Xan, who had recently perfected a spell to conjure light.

The crisp air made it easy to take a deep breath and brought a level of peace I had been craving. However, that feeling was short-lived as we followed a trail that led to a large clearing filled with people.

According to what we've been told, almost all the Harrison pack will be here tonight for the gathering, except for the children and some of the caregivers.

Riggs, now out of the suit, emerged from the shadows to approach us.

"I'm glad you decided to join us. I figured it might be interesting for you to see how the other half lives," he smirked in a way that made me like him even less. I swear the more time we spend in the presence of this alpha, the less charming he seems. Something about him feels unsettling.

I can't tell if what he said was meant to be a snub since we have pack gatherings occasionally and include the non-wolf members as well. The whole situation feels strange because he's the one who asked us to come here under the pretense of wanting us to help convince his council to integrate.

In this moment, I'm glad that Finley is our alpha and not me, she replies with tact and grace. "We wouldn't miss a chance to meet more of your lovely pack members and forge a deeper friendship.

Before moving closer to Riggs, she had been standing next to Xan. Judging by the narrowing of his eyes, he also finds the Harrison pack alpha unworthy. He moves to stand next to Finley in her new position, and the light at his fingertips flares brighter, illuminating more of the tree-shrouded area and giving an eerie glow to his face.

With his smirk blossoming into a full-blown grin, Riggs replies, "Well, let me show you around."

He guides us deeper into the clearing, weaving through the crowd of bodies, some human and others already in wolf form.

We pass a large bonfire surrounded by log seating. People are roasting marshmallows, drinking hot cocoa, and a couple with acoustic guitars is strumming an upbeat melody.

The popular hangout seemed to be tables filled with platters of food. Barbequed meats, cut fruit, and many other sides were laid out for the taking.

"Throughout the night, a variety of food will be available; feel free to help yourself whenever you're hungry." He gestured toward the tables. "Your visit coincides with one of the monthly open challenges for the alpha position, and I'd be overjoyed for you to witness it."

He stopped speaking and proceeded to lead us to what looked like a makeshift fighting ring. It wasn't the professional version you'd see when watching boxing or wrestling; this was more of an outline that had been left to the elements.

The crowd waiting around the ring parted to let us get closer, and Riggs walked directly into the square space.

One of the staff members we saw earlier approached with a megaphone. As he began to speak, the crowd around the clearing fell silent. "If anyone would like to challenge for the alpha position, now is the time to make your intentions known."

"I challenge Riggs," a man who must have been six and a half feet tall yelled as he stalked forward. With his size and the aggression radiating off him in waves, it felt as though the ground should tremble with each step he took.

A scoff emerged from a petite woman to my left. I turned to her as she stood, shaking her head with her arms crossed tightly over her chest.

When she saw me looking at her, I raised my eyebrow in question. She seemed to understand because she answered, "That's

Titus. Like clockwork, he challenges Riggs every month, and he loses every month."

"Is there conflict between them? It seems a bit foolish to continue challenging if he can't win," I said.

She shrugged, "They really are good friends, but he didn't believe Riggs should be alpha."

The man with the megaphone announced to the crowd that the fight was about to begin. Everyone quieted once more and moved forward to encircle the ring.

Both men removed their clothing and transformed before our eyes. Riggs turned into a sleek, muscular black wolf. He wasn't very large, but a dominant aura radiated from him. One eerie aspect was that when he turned his snout toward the crowd, his eyes became visible- bright and hauntingly yellow, a very rare trait among wolves. Titus, a golden wolf, on the other hand, was much larger than Riggs, standing at least a foot taller; while Riggs was muscled, Titus was simply bulky.

A bell tolled as the wolves began to stalk one another, neither seeming eager to make the first move. They paced and assessed, waiting for the perfect moment to strike.

Titus finally caved and lunged at Riggs, but his size made him slower. By the time he got close enough to Riggs to launch an attack, Riggs was already dodging away. In a flash, he was behind Titus, gripping his tail between his teeth, and with a jerk of his head, he tossed him to the other side of the ring.

Titus growled deeply and loudly before rising to his paws. Menace gleamed in his eyes as he approached the alpha, who didn't even bother to appear the least bit ruffled.

Returning to stalking each other, the crowd began calling out, jeering at the wolves, attempting to taunt them into action.

This time, Riggs mounted an attack. He ran full speed at Titus. At first, I thought it was foolish to attack his opponent head-first, but then, at the last minute, he slid on his belly, going under him. Raising his jaw upward, he bit Titus on the belly and clamped down.

A loud whine reverberated through the air as Titus flung himself backward, trying to wrench his stomach away from his attacker. Riggs refused to relent, pursuing him closely while still tightly gripping Titus.

Just when I thought things were getting good—maybe we'd finally see some bloodshed—the two detached and walked to opposite corners of the ring. They transformed back into men, as some of the bystanders approached to hand them clothing and rags to clean the dirt off themselves.

I complained more loudly than I intended, grumbling, "Why did they stop?"

Even though it wasn't directed at her, the woman behind me replied, "The alpha faces numerous challenges, so the council has mandated that the fights must end in submission rather than death. Otherwise, we would have already lost many good wolves. Titus communicated his withdrawal from the fight, but only pack members would have received it through our mental link."

My mood soured; I had hoped to see some violence, but now I was thoroughly disappointed.

We watched silently as three more challengers attempted and failed to defeat Riggs in a fight. Although he wasn't the largest wolf, he appeared to have a tactical mind. It was clear that his moves were deliberate rather than impulsive.

When no more opponents stepped forward, Riggs was confirmed as the reigning alpha once again. At the suggestion of those around us, we moved to the tables for some food.

Riggs and his assistant joined our group. He had put on pants but remained shirtless, and seeing how sweaty he was, I couldn't blame him. The chilly night air should help him cool off soon enough.

A basket of smoked meats was passed around, followed by side dishes, and we all filled our plates.

"What'd you think?" Riggs asked with a twinkle in his eye as he stuffed a glob of potato salad into his mouth.

"It was interesting," Alder replied. For those who didn't know him, the response would suffice, but I could tell he didn't find it interesting at all.

Finley responded next, "I believe it would become tiresome to do that every month."

"Don't think you can handle it?" he goaded her.

With a growl, she replied, "I didn't say that. I just believe it would get old quickly, always being aware that someone is rooting for you to fail. Always needing to watch your back. It would be difficult to view your pack as a family in that kind of environment."

I decided to add my two cents: "I guess it's not surprising to fight the same opponents month after month when you only fight to submission rather than death."

"Is that how you believe they should be handled?"

"Yes," I said. "I believe anyone might make a foolish decision once if their heart is in the right place. However, repeating such a mistake shows a lack of loyalty to you."

"Oh, your second is vicious," Riggs directed at Finley. "I like it," he said more quietly, glancing in my direction.

My nose wrinkled in response, while a growl emerged from Alder, who sat beside me.

Don't ask me why I did it, but in that moment, feeling the energy he was emitting, I slid my hand under the picnic table and gently rested it on Al's thigh.

He appeared to calm at my touch, yet he didn't shift his glare from the alpha.

"What about you, Sasquatch?" he asked.

"What about me?" Alder responded hesitantly.

"Do you ever fight?"

"I can fight, but I prefer to do so only when necessary."

"Hmm." Riggs tapped his fingertips against his jaw for a moment, simply staring at Alder. "I'd like to spar with you."

Alder quickly and politely declined the request.

"I insist!" Riggs exclaimed. "Pardon my rudeness; it's just that I've never met a sasquatch before. I'd very much like to see your beast form and discover what you can do."

I could tell Al was uncomfortable with the proposition, but the alpha was insistent and eventually, my squatch gave in.

"Just sparring," he said.

"Yes, yes," the alpha replied, waving him off. "Let's give them a show, shall we?"

Riggs snapped his fingers a couple of times in quick succession, and a pair of women approached. He instructed them to clean up after our group, which made me uncomfortable. It wouldn't have taken long for us to put away our own plates and trash. I've never known Finley to request such menial tasks of pack members; we were family rather than monarch and subject.

Riggs once again stripped off his pants; this time, he maintained eye contact with me and winked in my direction. Gross.

My big guy growled, and I turned toward him. In the past, I wouldn't have cared about his feelings, but now that I had accepted our bond as mates, I knew he needed to control his emotions before entering the ring; otherwise, he was likely to get hurt by charging in recklessly.

I gazed into his deep green eyes. A feeling of home enveloped me. My hand seemed to have a mind of its own as it wove through the wavy brown strands of his hair. Gripping his head, I brought the giant down to my level and planted a kiss on his lips.

Despite the one time we hooked up many months ago, this was new, so I kept the kiss to a quick peck. The kiss seemed to take him by surprise, and he froze, almost like he was glitching. When I turned away, my wrist was grabbed, and I found myself being swung back around.

Alder yanked me toward him, my body colliding with his. He kissed me back this time, and with a hum resonating from deep in his chest, he nipped at my bottom lip.

A look of determination shone in his eyes as he released me.

The plaid shirt he wore was removed, followed by the t-shirt underneath. His chest was fully exposed, and I had to give myself a little shake before doing something stupid like drooling. At around six foot four, there was nothing small about the squatch. He wasn't cut with muscles, but he was solid. I couldn't help where my thoughts wandered as I imagined running my fingers through the smattering of hair that trailed down his chest.

The next second, my gentle giant transformed into his squatch form, which stood at least a foot taller and was much bulkier. The sweatpants he had kept on now looked like a child's pants as they rode up to mid-calf.

Since they were not part of the same pack, they couldn't communicate mind to mind. Therefore, if one wanted to forfeit the sparring match, they were to hit the ground three times.

Once the person volunteering as a referee reviewed the rules, they climbed into the ring.

The bell rang, indicating it was time to fight, and Riggs wasted no time going on the offensive—an interesting tactic since he was used to facing the same opponents repeatedly, whereas Alder was entirely new. If I were in his position, I'd test the waters, perhaps allowing my opponent to make a few moves so I could size them up.

When Riggs came within arm's reach of Alder, he was swatted away like a gnat, sliding across the ground.

Undeterred, he charged again, this time attempting to bite at my squatch's ankles. I couldn't help but chuckle as Alder hooked his leg under the wolf and punted him to the other side of the ring.

This went on and on, with Riggs trying to launch an attack while Alder thwarted every attempt to get close. Finally, after what was likely thirty minutes, the wolf stomped his foot three times.

When the referee called the fight to an end, Riggs changed back into his human form and sat panting on the ground.

He regarded Alder with a newly gained air of respect.

Alder's squatch was clearly unimpressed as he turned away from the fallen man and walked off, his leg lifting high enough to clear the ring's ropes.

I began to wonder why he wasn't changing back just as he reached me, and with one swift motion, tossed me over his shoulder.

"What the hell?" I shouted.

All I received in return was a grumble and a firm paw to my backside.

"Have fun, kids!" Xan shouted before doubling over with laughter.

Twenty

KAI

While my wolf reveled in being manhandled, I was not pleased to be indignantly hauled around like a sack of potatoes. My fists met hard muscles as I pounded on my mate's back. He remained completely unfazed as he marched us back to the mansion, up the stairs, and to our assigned room, stopping only to growl at anyone who tried to get in his way.

A thrill surged within me at his gruff possessiveness, allowing nothing to interfere with his desires. I could easily become accustomed to this side of him—it was intoxicating.

When he entered our room, Alder had to stoop down; his squatch form was well over seven feet tall, and this room was not made to accommodate someone of his size. He didn't let it affect him as he crossed the room and unceremoniously tossed me onto the bed.

An oomph escaped me as I hit the mattress.

My beastie inched closer to me, a wild glint in his eyes.

Those giant paws of his grabbed my ankles and dragged me to the edge. All I could do was watch in fascination, my wolf howling in delight. The way he was handling me made me realize that maybe there was more to my mate, who often had the sweetness of a cinnamon roll.

With swift movements, my joggers and top were pulled from my body, leaving me in just my undergarments.

He was reaching for the waistband of my panties when I smacked his paw. He halted his movements, turning his face to look at me. A low growl vibrated in his throat, followed by an animalist, "Mine." That was the most coherent statement I have ever heard from his beast form.

"Yes, yours, but not like this."

There was grumbling from the beast, but I crossed my arms, holding firm. When he merely stared at me with an agitated aura, I said, "This isn't going any further until you change back."

He stomped a foot on the ground while pouting, causing the contents of the room to shake. Each of his feet in beast form was longer than my forearm.

I understood that this version of Alder represented his most primal self, and he likely felt rejected by my request to restore his human side, but there was no way I would engage in any intimate activities like this.

Grasping one of his paws, I held it gently between my hands, stroking the skin softly. I waited until he looked at me again, ensuring he could see my sincerity. "I know you care about me;

I care about you too. But I need you to bring your human back. It wouldn't work between us like this, Big Guy."

He huffed, and I swear it sounded like grudging agreement before his entire body shivered and shook, revealing Alder in his human form.

His eyes grew comically wide as he realized the situation, he found himself in. He gulped as he took me in, laying on the bed in just my bra and panties.

He stammered as he tried to say something, but he never managed to get it out.

Rising from the bed, I approached him with the grace of a predator. My shy mate was back, but I had already decided we would not go back to pretending to be strangers.

It's been several months since our explosive tryst in the study, and we weren't naked then. Now that we are giving this mating a chance, I'm ready for more.

I approached him with graceful movements. "Why are you still dressed?"

When I stood toe to toe with him, I see his cheeks pinken, quickly turning crimson. It isn't the behavior I'm accustomed to from my previous partners, but I can't help finding it cute- a feeling I never would have anticipated before.

I removed the sweatpants he was wearing and raised a brow upon discovering his lack of boxers, which was unexpected.

Standing before him, I appraise his body. His light beige skin appears smooth and unblemished, only interrupted in places by hair. He has bulky muscles rather than being defined and sharp-angled. I must admit to myself that I find the prospect appealing—he's strong yet also soft, probably perfect for cuddling against. The thought of cuddling makes me feel disgusted with myself as soon as I consider it. Who am I becoming? After I chide myself, I decide to worry about it later; I have more interesting things on my mind right now.

There's dirt on his legs and elbows from the sparring he did in his squatch form. A shower will remedy the mess, but it may also help move things along He was confident in his plans for me until he transformed; now, the self-consciousness of man is hindering our progress.

Knowing I must approach this with caution, I gently grasp his hand.

"Let's get you all cleaned up, big guy."

I guide him to the bathroom attached to our room and adjust the shower to a comfortable temperature. When I think it's right, I nudge him toward the shower, and he steps in without protest.

He watches me with uncertainty, but his expression quickly shifts to one of desire as I remove my bra and panties.

I step into the shower behind him and lather my hands with body wash. I begin at his neck and shoulders, applying soothing strokes against his skin. Gliding my fingertips down the taut muscles of his shoulders, along his thick arms, to his fingers. I massage his back in circular motions. I move my hand lower, cupping his ass and giving it a squeeze. It's quite firm, and my wolf howls inside, yearning to bite it. He already has a bite mark from the mating ceremony, so this would be solely for my pleasure. I might do it eventually, but I'm suppressing the feeling for now. I don't want to frighten him away tonight.

When I turn him around, I gather more soap and continue my ministrations. My hands trail down his chest and further. Down, down, down. Scrubbing through the trail of hair that intersects his chest and leads lower to his cock, which is standing hard at attention.

Touching him, however gently, is getting me wet, and I want to touch him in a way that I know will lead us to intimacy, but first, I need to finish my task. I quickly finish washing his legs and feet.

Once my mate is clean, I spray him off and, using some more of the woodsy-scented body wash, wrap my hand around his shaft and start working it up and down. Stroking him with firm jerks.

"You don't have to—" he begins, but I interrupt him.

"I want to."

In just a few minutes, he twitches and grunts as he comes against my palm.

Before I know his intentions, he drops to his knees. His head bows forward, and drops of water slide down his face, interrupting the intensity. I don't think I've ever seen a more beautiful sight.

"What are you doing?" I ask him, biting my lip to keep my thoughts to myself.

His calloused hands encircle my thighs. The left one is lifted and tossed over his shoulder. The position exposes my core, putting it on full display for him. I know precisely what he's seeing. I'm a dripping mess from being aroused by the attention I gave him.

A soft groan of approval escapes him before he brings his mouth to my center. He starts softly licking my clit, stroking it tentatively, testing my reaction. When I begin to get into it, he increases his pressure. Licking, lapping, swirling his tongue, bringing me pure carnal pleasure.

My hand finds itself in the wet curls of his long hair, gripping him tightly to me as if, subconsciously, I'm afraid he'll try to escape before bringing me the relief I'm desperately seeking.

With an explosion of ecstasy, I come, trembling against his soft lips. He continues to swipe his tongue against my core until I'm spent, and there's no remaining evidence of the mess I made.

Using my grip on his hair, I tug him to his feet. The heat in his eyes reveals just how much he enjoys the rough treatment.

Our mouths collide in a fiercely passionate kiss. My legs wrap around him as he fumbles with the knobs on the wall, turning off the water. Using one foot, I push the shower door open while he carries us back to the bedroom.

We don't bother to dry off, water dripping everywhere as he leads us to the bed. The mess we're creating will be a concern for another time.

He sits on the edge of the bed, positioning me to straddle his lap.

I'm somewhat surprised when he reaches through my legs from behind. Rubbing my core lightly, making a moan slip from me.

His stubbled beard brushes my skin, creating a delightful contrast to his tender kisses on my neck. Teeth scrape across my collarbone as he asks, "Are you going to use me, little wolf?" His question is accompanied by the upward thrust of his hips, causing his erection to rub against me. "I'm yours for the taking, eternally at your service. Your willing supplicant, ready to worship at the altar of your flesh."

I'm still throbbing from my recent orgasm, but I want what he's offering me. Gripping his cock, I guide it home. My leg muscles tense and strain as I move, rocking against him.

"So wet for me," he purrs with his mouth against my ear. The wisp of air tickles and sends a skittering sensation of tingles along my neck.

His hands grip tightly on my hips as he directs my movements, raising me up and forcing me back down. Impaling me with his large shaft. The thickness spreads me wide.

Moans escape my lips as I quiver with pleasure.

Hours pass as we meld into one. The experience is shockingly intense; it has never been like this with anyone else, and I know it is because I have accepted what fate has designed for me. We get to spend the rest of forever reveling in this feeling. My heart feels as if it stuttered to a stop, and when it begins to beat again, it only does so for him. The last thought I have before sleep claims me is that I am truly a goner.

Twenty-One

ALDER

"*Wake up.*" I hear a melodious voice floating to me in my sleep.

I'm far too comfortable to wake up now. After Kai and I had our fill of each other, we drifted off to sleep curled together. For such a gruff and intimidating woman, I thought with near certainty that she would have no interest in cuddling. I could almost imagine her voice saying, "disgusting," as her button nose crinkled in distaste. But she proved me wrong.

The smell of her clings to me in this dream realm. It is most likely a result of my not-so-subtle attempts to fill my lungs with her scent, taking deep breaths of her hair last night.

Just as I sigh in contentment, a firm poke in my chest causes me to wince. Dang, that was a sensitive area.

"Wake up." This time, I realize it isn't just my overtired musings that I heard earlier. It's real.

"Alder. Wake up, now," Kai says, sounding even more panicked. This time, thankfully, she accompanied it with a shoulder shake rather than another stab to my peck.

I crack my eyes open reluctantly. It takes a minute for my eyes to adjust to the dim lighting. They focus on Kai as she raises her pointer finger to her lips, shushing me before I open my mouth.

My brow furrows in concern. At first, I hoped the abrupt awakening was due to her renewed interest in going another round between the sheets, but when I caught a glimpse of her face, I knew that was not the case. Clearly, something is wrong. *Not now*, I tell my dick. I will it to settle down, there will be other times.

Since she doesn't want me to speak, I furrow my brows, trying to convey 'what's wrong'.

She brings her mouth as close to my ear as possible and whispers, "Get dressed. Something is wrong."

She doesn't have to tell me twice. I quickly put on the clothes I wore earlier to the pack party. I got pretty sweaty before, so I wish I had a change of clothes; however, since we hadn't planned to stay the night, we don't have overnight bags.

Once we are both dressed, I walk toward her, only to freeze when I hear the gentle jiggle of the doorknob. Despite my sasquatch's desire to be with our mate earlier, the beast thankfully locked the door. Even with this primitive mindset, he wouldn't have wanted anyone else to see what belongs only to us.

At that thought, I give my primal side an imaginary high five before shaking off the lustful thoughts. Whoever is trying to get in won't be kept out forever, just long enough to find a key or pick the lock.

While we didn't take time to enjoy it earlier, I'm thankful we saw the balcony attached to our room. It's going to come in handy.

Kai must be thinking the same thing as I am because she walks silently across the room to it. She leaves the long curtains in place but slides the glass door open.

We stealthily slide out and shut the door behind us. Walking the length of the balcony, which I noticed earlier wraps around two-thirds of the house, we move as silently as possible, only stopping when we've counted the number of windows it took to arrive at Finley and Xan's room.

Taking a deep breath, I tap on the glass. The longer we go unanswered, the louder and more insistent I become. It would be unwise to be loud if we want to avoid detection, but escaping does us no good if our alpha and my best friend are left behind.

A thump resonates from inside the room, followed by footsteps approaching in our direction.

The curtain slides open, but without interior lights on, it's hard to see who is at the window. Before the sliding glass is pulled open, a muttered curse that sounds distinctly like Xan is heard.

"What are you doing?" he grumbles, standing before us in only his underwear, his face groggy with sleep and his dark hair mussed.

A growl erupts from deep within my chest before my hand shoots up to cover Kai's eyes, blocking her view of my best friend's nude skin.

"Relax, caveman," Kai grumbles, swatting my hand away.

"Sorry," I mumble, grateful for the semi-darkness around us, which helps conceal the blush I know is creeping into my cheeks from embarrassment. "My squatch really didn't like the idea of you seeing another male mostly nude, even if it's my best friend." I look away, avoiding eye contact.

Her palm caresses my stubbled cheek as her lips hover near my ear. "I have no interest in seeing him, and if that isn't enough to quell your beast, how about the fact that I still smell like you?" Her eyebrow arches as she smirks at me.

My chest rises at the thought of her scent revealing our illicit activities to anyone within smelling distance of her.

Nodding my head in concession, I shove Xan backward, allowing space for us to enter the room.

Kai shuts the door behind us, and Xan, who hasn't moved to cover himself, stands before us, pinching the bridge of his nose. "You know it's the middle of the night, right? And why are you coming in from the balcony?"

"Yes, captain, it's obvious. We are aware of the time." Kai shoots him a dirty look before crossing the room to where Finley is still sleeping. I'm not sure how she hasn't woken up from all the noise Xan made getting out of bed.

"Hey, wake up," Kai whispers, gently shaking Finley's shoulder. It's interesting that she wakes Fin up much more gently than she woke me.

Noticing the pile of clothes on the floor beside me, I scoop them up and toss them at Xan. "Get dressed," I tell him.

When Kai pesters her sufficiently, Finley ultimately wakes up. She sits up slowly and gazes around the room in confusion.

"We need to go," Kai tells her.

Xan nearly trips as he struggles to put on his jeans. I give him an annoyed glance, allowing him to see my exasperation. "Shh."

"What's happening?" Finley asks.

"Something is wrong, and we need to leave," Kai explains before I can speak.

Finley accepts her words unquestioningly. It's evident that she trusts her in her role as second in command.

"Kai woke me a few minutes ago because she had a bad feeling. I was getting dressed when someone tried to open our room door. We used the wraparound balcony to evade whoever was trying to enter our room."

Once our alpha and her mate are ready, we head to the door. Xan rummages through his bag for a moment before producing a pouch. "Let me go first; I'll check down the hall quickly, and I'll return to let you know if the coast is clear."

A noise comes from Finley; I think she plans to argue about her mate going first, but before she can, he plants a firm kiss on her lips and opens the door.

We stand in silence that lingers for far too long, but glancing at my watch, it's only a few minutes before the door reopens. A dark head of hair appears as Xan pops back in.

"It's clear," he says, gesturing for us to follow him.

Twenty-Two

KAI

X an and I had a minor argument about who should go first. Both of us wanted to protect Finley—Xan motivated by their mate bond and I motivated by her being my best friend and my pack alpha. Eventually, I conceded.

We determined that it would be best for Finley to be positioned between us, which upset her.

"You two act like I'm defenseless," she growled, her wolf fangs glinting in the low light. She raised her hands, spread wide, revealing that she had transformed them into claws as well.

Grabbing her shoulders, Xan turned her to him and said, "We know, love. You're one of the baddest of the bad." His eyes were sincere, indicating he spoke the truth. "We both just feel the need to protect you, even if it's not rational."

I gave her a firm pat on the shoulder, hoping it conveyed all my thoughts on the matter—she was important to us, we knew she could defend herself, but she also had us.

"We should go," Alder reminded us. "We don't know if whoever was at our door has managed to get inside yet. They might already know we're missing."

Xan took the lead, holding aloft a pouch of something magical. Finley trailed closely behind him, followed by Alder and me bringing up the rear.

While I might have argued to take the lead, which I felt was suitable for my position in the pack, I could also say I was relieved it worked out this way. Walking in my place kept me near Finley so I could uphold my duty, while also allowing me to be close to my mate. I would defend him as well, if necessary.

The hallway lighting was scarce, with only a few lamps on a dim setting, shown every few feet.

We crept quietly down the stairway without encountering anyone else. A creeping sense of unease settled like a cloak around my shoulders, making the hairs on my arms stand on end.

With no interference, we quickly exited the front door of the property into the chill of the night. Taking a quick look at the darkened sky, I saw that there was no moon to be seen. I vaguely remember seeing it when we were at the pack party Riggs hosted, but now it was nowhere to be seen.

That unsettling feeling began to feel like stones in my gut. Something was profoundly wrong.

When we paused outside the door to assess our surroundings, I elbowed Xan. "Did you notice the moon's disappearing act?"

His brow furrowed as he gazed at the sky. "I don't see it, but I think we have bigger things to worry about."

I rolled my eyes and turned toward Finley. "Sometimes, I question your mating with this male. He can be rather dense."

Finley flashed a secret smile before turning to her mate to explain.

"The absence of the moon is a problem. While shifters don't need the moon to access our other form, its absence will diminish our powers. Our strength will be significantly reduced."

His expression changed from confusion to anger upon hearing the news. "So, you think it was intentional? Do you believe that someone with magic is interfering in some way?"

"That is my theory, yes," I replied. "Which is why I am pointing it out."

"We need to be especially cautious," Finley remarked.

"Damn it," Xan cursed, fiercely stamping his foot.

"What?" Alder asked.

"Yesterday, when we all went to our rooms to settle in, they asked me to move the car. It's parked all the way on the other side of the property."

No one appeared to take the news well, but there wasn't much that could be done about it.

"Do you happen to have one of those netty things in your bag?" I asked him.

"Actually, I do!" he replied, rummaging in his bag. Once he found it, he quickly helped cover Alder for the trek.

He thanked us both, but his expression told me how much it meant to him that I was concerned for his health and safety.

"We better get moving; lead the way," I instructed Xan.

He performed his new magic trick, creating little orbs of light in his palms. He sent one towards each of us, hovering above our heads. He kept one for himself and held the pouch aloft, ready for any threats that might reveal themselves.

We followed him into a slightly wooded area as his mate teased him. When Finley went on her first date with him, he took her to a secluded field at night with the intention of having a picnic by a waterfall. However, Finley was unaware of their destination and felt uneasy about being taken to a pitch-dark field in the middle of nowhere with a man she had just met. She poked fun at him, joking that if he had mastered this light trick back then, she wouldn't have thought he was a murderer while he rummaged around in his trunk for a flashlight.

His response was related to hindsight and everything that entails.

"I was quite annoyed with you after that date," I pointed out to Finley.

"I remember. You didn't outright berate me, but I could tell you really wanted to." She huffed.

"Honestly, I knew it was your first date from that dating app Mate Match, but I assumed you had enough street smarts to choose a public place for the meeting. At least he wasn't an axe murderer, and things turned out fine." I shrugged.

"Yes, everything turned out perfectly. I found my mate, and I managed to delete that dreadful app."

"What was so dreadful?" I asked with genuine curiosity.

"The number of unsolicited dick pics that ended up in my inbox."

I had to cover my mouth to contain the bark of laughter that escaped me. "Yeah, I learned early on to never open a picture message there. Ninety-nine percent of the time, they were dick photos. Sorry I failed to warn you."

Xan, now facing us while leading, wore an expression I couldn't quite read in the dim lighting and asked, "Hypothetically, if someone's account happened to reactivate, would their previous messages still be linked to their account?"

Finley seemed to be considering the idea, but it was clear that I understood quicker than the rest of our group where this 'hypothetical' question was leading. Despite our need for secrecy, I couldn't help but let a laugh escape from me.

"Oh, that's perfect," I said with a wide smile in his direction.

A look of pure malice crossed his features, and Finley must have finally caught on to his intentions. She swatted him on the arm with an, "Whatever is going through your head right now, stop thinking about it. You need to forget it."

He tried to embody innocence as he pretended not to know what she was getting at.

"Ignore her. Whatever mayhem you're planning, I want in," I said as I offered him a fist bump. It wasn't often that we found ourselves on the same side of an issue, but I would wholeheartedly back him on this. Having received several such pictures, I decided that whatever scheming he was up to was well deserved.

Alder surprised me by pitching in, "It seems fair game if they were slimy enough to send unsuspecting victims photos of their manhood."

Finley was the only one in our group who opposed Xan's scheming. She believed the past should remain in the past. Xan made eye contact with me and silently mouthed, "We'll talk later." His accompanying grin was downright feral.

Xan informed us that we were getting closer, saying, "If I remember correctly—which I hope I do for our sake—it should be only another half mile or so."

No sooner had the words left his mouth than we were met with trouble.

A growl emanated from the cluster of trees ahead of us. It wasn't long before a dozen pairs of glowing eyes became visible. At the forefront of the group was a large black wolf, its yellow eyes alight with malice—Riggs.

My chest rattled with a growl of my own. He obviously had some sort of ulterior motives for us visiting his pack lands. Whoever tried getting into our room must have done so under his orders.

"Going somewhere?" Celeste asked, approaching from behind the Harrison alpha. What the hell was she doing here?

"Celeste." Xan sneered at her with disdain. "What did we do to deserve your unpleasant presence?"

"You have something of mine," she replied, glancing past me at Alder.

I took a threatening step closer to their group, saying, "There's nothing of yours here."

Riggs transformed back into his human form. Unfortunately, he was completely naked, with his flaccid penis exposed. Gross.

"What do they have?" he asked her.

"That awful blonde woman stole my mate," she shouted, pointing an accusatory finger at me.

The growl that escaped from me could only be seen as having lethal intent. I would not allow her to get away with it.

He pouted in Celeste's direction. "What are you talking about, lovely? We're mates." He gestured between them.

A cringe-worthy cackle escaped from Celeste before she rolled her eyes and referred to him as an imbecile. However, the alpha continued to insist that they were mates and that she was simply confused.

"It seems like another victim of her love potions," Xan whispered.

"I could say this has been fun, but I'd prefer not to lie. So, if you could please step aside, we'll be on our way," Finley told them.

Celeste began shouting for them to detain us, and while Riggs was convinced she was merely confused about Alder, he directed his wolves to capture us.

Despite our powers being dampened by the absence of the moon, it didn't take too long for Finley and me to transform into wolves. With a roar of anger, Alder morphed into his Squatch form.

With a rip of fabric, he pushed his arms through the material that covered him. If we weren't in a dire situation, I would've taken the time to point out the absurdity of seeing a seven-foot beast wearing the mosquito net over his body. I'll have to comment on it later when we are no longer in imminent danger.

The snarling minions accompanying Riggs started to approach us.

"Not so fast," Xan yelled as he tossed the pouch he had been carrying. I had forgotten he even possessed the thing, whatever it was.

It quickly became evident that it had created some sort of smoke cover. Once it started spreading, it was impossible to see our advisories, which hopefully meant they were also unable to see us.

His hand shot out, amplifying our personal light orbs and prompting the charge toward the car.

Unfortunately, we didn't get far. Celeste counteracted Xan's magic, causing the smoke to dissipate. We were now worse off than before, as we were standing closer to the others.

One of the wolves broke the invisible boundary between us and appeared to be headed straight towards me. I braced my paws in the dirt, preparing to stand my ground, but before he could descend upon me, a long, muscular arm covered in fur swung between us, sending the wolf flying several feet into the air.

Al roared in anger and outrage, his beast clearly triggered by the enemy attempting to attack his mate.

Madness descended upon the entire population in the woods. Celeste and Xan faced off against one another, casting spells at each other, going blow-for-blow with no clear winner in sight.

The wolves charged at us, jaws open and fangs poised to tear flesh from our bodies.

We confronted them directly despite being outnumbered. My teeth clashed with my enemy's bodies as we fiercely tore into one another.

More often than not, we were the dominant force, but the lack of moonlight was affecting all of us wolves. Injuries were sustained on both sides.

Deep growls rumbled from a direction different from that of the group we had been fighting.

I turned my muzzle to assess the newest threat. I saw a pack of wolves coming in our direction, led by a large golden wolf, almost the size of the alpha. It took only a moment to realize it was Titus—the wolf that frequently challenged Riggs for the alpha position.

At first, we prepared to be even more outnumbered, but Titus quickly changed to human form and addressed our group.

"Run! We'll hold them back," he shouted before transforming into his wolf form again and rushing towards his alpha to confront him and the madwoman, Celeste.

We sprinted as if our lives depended on it—which they absolutely did. Finley, who was the least injured, carried her mate on her back since the warlock couldn't run as fast as our wolves.

Thanks were given to the fates as we shifted back into our human bodies and climbed into the vehicle. Xan took the driver's seat, and I wouldn't argue with him about it. I was too hurt to do so.

The car roared to life as the gas pedal was pressed to the floor.

Twenty-Three

ALDER

We safely reached the highway leading away from the Harrison pack lands, but we were worse for wear. Most of us had at least minor injuries. Kai had a large cut on her shoulder. I'm not sure if it was from claws or fangs, but either way, it would need thorough disinfecting and stitches.

I removed my shirt and turned it inside out to avoid any dirt that might linger from our skirmish. Holding it to her shoulder, I cursed as the blood soaked through.

"What are we going to do?" I asked anxiously.

Her wounds needed tending, and the blood accumulating was making my squatch frantic. It was hard to focus with him panicking in my head.

As a shifter, she couldn't go to a human hospital; she would need at least a healer with magical abilities, but possibly someone more skilled than that.

Xan directed me to hand over my cellphone to Finley. After digging it out of my back pocket with one hand, I did so.

She turned back to me, holding it up in front of my face to unlock it.

"Okay, what do I need to do?" she asked.

She may be the alpha of our pack, but this is her best friend who is injured. With her nerves frayed, she allows Xan to take the lead for the moment.

"Retrieve the contact information for the agent at the International Bureau of Magical Enforcement. Call him and set it to speaker mode."

She followed his instructions with shaky hands.

As the phone rang a few times, my mind was filled with curse words and silent prayers to the fates. When I started to feel hopeless about the situation, the call was answered.

"This is Agent Schaffer."

Xan took over. "Hello, this is Alexander Moretti, mate to the Fang alpha. You might not remember me in particular, but I was at the meeting you had with Alder Waldvogel about the witch Celeste Blackmore you are currently looking for."

"Ah yes, I remember. I'm surprised to hear from you instead of Mr. Waldvogel or Alpha Thomson. How can I assist you?"

"They're here with me but indisposed," he stated, and we expressed our agreement. "We are currently in Kentucky. We came here to meet with the Harrison pack. We were lured here under the pretense of them wanting to enact a mixed pack structure like ours and sought our expertise on the idea. We stayed the night to attend an event they were hosting and woke to an attack. Their leader aligned himself with Celeste."

Agent Schaffer asked whether we had gotten away and what our location was.

"We were heavily outnumbered and might not have escaped without the help of some pack members who turned against their leader. We are currently on the highway just a few minutes away—for all I know, they could be following closely behind us. We have all sustained some minor injuries, but Kai needs urgent medical attention."

Schaffer instructed Xan about a location we could reach within thirty minutes, but I could no longer focus on the conversation when my injured mate whimpered in pain.

"Hold on, baby. We're on our way to help." I pressed the shirt firmly against her shoulder, torn inside knowing that the pressure surely hurt, but also aware that if she lost too much blood, this could become a critical injury.

With my free hand, I pushed back her matted hair and kissed her forehead. "I've got you."

My eyes welled with tears. Fates, I hoped that wouldn't be a lie.

Twenty-Four

ALDER

The house Agent Schaffer directed us to was supposed to be about a thirty-minute drive away. I needed to get an award for Xan when all of this was over; my best friend really came through for me, getting us there in twenty minutes.

We followed a dirt driveway that ended in a small cottage house. The porch was well lit, and I could see a woman waiting there. She looked to be in her mid- to late sixties, but since she was some sort of supernatural, there really was no telling how old she was. If she had the experience and skills necessary to help Kai, then her age didn't matter to me the least.

We all opened our doors and hustled to the house. I scooped Kai into my arms and carried her to the woman who assessed us, bundling her long white hair at the nape of her neck.

"Follow the hallway to the last door on the left; that's the exam room," she instructed.

It wasn't too large of a space, but it seemed to be well equipped.

I laid Kai on the metal examination table that had a paper covering on top. If I weren't worried about her bleeding out, I'd feel more frustrated by how uncomfortable it looked for her.

"You two will need to go wait somewhere else," she said, pointing to Finley and Xan. You can rest in the living room, or if you're hungry, you can help yourself to anything in the kitchen."

Finley attempted to speak object while the healer washed and sanitized her hands but was ultimately overruled by the older woman.

"The room is too small," she gestured around the space.

Finley finally left clearly dejected after Xan ushered her out the door.

"Please tell me what happened."

As she cut off Kai's torn sleeve to examine the injury, I told her everything.

She walked to a drawer across the room and returned with several vials of various potions. I wasn't certain what they were, but I had to trust that she knew what she was doing.

One pink-colored potion was poured on the wound before being dabbed with a cotton ball. Kai cried out in pain from the contact of the liquid with her cut. I hated this; if I could take the pain for her, I would do it in a heartbeat- no second thoughts needed.

She removed the stopper from a concoction that looked like green sludge before handing it to me.

I was instructed, "She needs to drink that one; help her get it down. She can't spit it out."

Getting her to swallow it was difficult, and I couldn't blame her for her reaction. It was thick, green, and smelled dreadful.

After several swallows that led to gagging, which I soothed her through, the vial was finally empty. I handed it back to the healer, who placed it in a bin by the sink.

"That one was intended to prevent any infections that might have been transmitted by the wolf that injured her."

I tried not to, but I couldn't hold back a wince when a powdery substance was sprinkled on the wound. It had to be painful, yet it seemed to have stopped the bleeding. I stroked Kai's hair repeatedly while the healer worked.

After applying a numbing agent, she began stitching. It required a great many stitches. As each one was added, I silently vowed that no one would ever harm my mate again.

Once the stitches were finished, a gauze wrap was added. We sat in silence while the healer cleaned up her supplies, and I held Kai close in my arms. I wasn't ready to let go of her yet, and she didn't seem ready either.

A quick knock resonated at the door before it swung open. Xan poked his head in to inform us that Agent Schaffer had arrived.

As gently as I could, I picked up Kai and followed Xan to the living room, where the others waited for us.

We passed a clock in the hallway, and I was surprised to see that a few hours had passed since we arrived at the house. It felt impossible, but I confirmed the time was correct when I sat down on the couch.

Agent Schaffer greeted us and reintroduced his partner, Laramie.

"We were also out of state and managed to reroute our flight back when you called. A local team was dispatched to the Harrison pack lands as soon as we hung up the phone."

"You've caught her?" Xan asked, his eyes betraying a mix of hope and malice.

The look that crossed Schaffer's face made my stomach drop.

"Unfortunately, no."

A barrage of curses erupted from most of the room's occupants.

If I didn't have Kai in my lap, I would've been on my feet at the news. Whether that would have been to intimidate the agents for their failures or to hunt for Celeste myself, I can't tell.

"How the fuck did that happen?" Xan voiced what we all wondered through clenched teeth.

Schaffer settled into the armchair across from me. He didn't answer immediately, but when he finally did, his regret seemed genuine.

"The local team arrived on scene within forty minutes. It's the best we could do considering the distance from the office. She was already gone. We were also unable to find the pack alpha, Riggs. He seems to have disappeared when Celeste got away. Someone named Titus has been named as the interim alpha. He assisted our agents with access to the grounds and helped with interviewing pack members. When they entered

Riggs's sleeping quarters, they found evidence that Celeste had stayed there with him and several empty potion bottles. Several members of the pack have voiced their concerns about Riggs's recent uncharacteristic behavior and the possibility of him being affected by a love potion. Based on what we were told and her penchant for love potions, we agree. We've sent the empty potion bottles to our labs for testing, with orders to expedite the results."

With the love potion theory seeming to be most likely true, I had to ask, "If she is using potions on other supernaturals, why does she still care about getting to me?"

"Honestly, it doesn't make much sense," Laramie agreed.

Schaffer shifted in his seat, making eye contact with me specifically. "When she fled the Harrison property, she did get away, but she left her belongings behind, so we have those collected for evidence as well. They're still reviewing the contents, but they found some pretty disturbing items. We don't know why, but she seems fixated on you. She wrote extensively about you in a journal we found."

"So, this is probably not the last time we'll encounter her?" Finley asked.

"Unfortunately, I don't believe so. Things have escalated significantly, and we are very concerned about your safety and that of your pack. We had a brief discussion about it on our way here. We think it would be best to bring you into our witness protection. It's similar to what the United States government does for humans, but since the supernatural community is much smaller, it is an international program. Of course, we would allow your mate to come with you."

I couldn't do anything for a minute except stare in stunned silence at the agents. They wanted me to enter a supernatural version of witness protection, where I could end up in who knows which country. My head was already shaking in refusal.

Schaffer raised a hand in a calming gesture. "I know that sounds extreme, but Celeste is proving to be a much tougher witch to capture, and she has numerous resources and connections. If you were to enter the program, we believe the risk to your pack would be minimal."

"Minimal risk is not the same as no risk," Xan remarked.

"How long will they need to be in the program?" Finley asked.

"There's not really a way for us to determine that at this point. First, we would need to capture Celeste; then, we would have to get everything sorted out for a trial. Once the trial takes place, we would need you to testify. If she is found guilty—which she should be—I'd probably recommend going back to the program for a minimum of six months just to ensure that she doesn't use any assistance on the outside to retaliate against you."

This was an outright nightmare. We were asked to go to an unknown location, have no contact with our pack or family, and also had no idea how long to expect. Obviously, one of us being killed or severely injured by Celeste would be worse, but that didn't make this choice feel any better.

As much as I hated the possibility, I would do it to ensure that Kai and my pack family were kept safe. Well, hopefully, they would be safe when we left. the agents didn't even sound too confident about that.

Did they know anything at all?

Feeling defeated, I was about to reluctantly agree with the agents—as long as Kai was okay with it. However, Finley beat me to an answer.

"Thank you for the offer, but they will be staying with us."

She looked at Xan with a questioning expression, almost as if silently asking if he agreed, which he verbalized when he said, "We are safer in numbers and, therefore, stronger together."

Schaffer and Laramie exchanged a worried glance but didn't comment on it at first.

My mate, who had been quietly nestled against my chest, sat up with my assistance and spoke to them.

"I agree. It would be safer for us to stay together, especially since you can't guarantee *anything at all*."

From the sass in her tone, it seemed she must have been feeling a bit better than she had when we arrived at the cottage. The healer did a good job. Before we left today, I needed to make sure we got her contact information and sent her something when we got home. What do you gift the person who saves your mate's life? A fruit basket? A restaurant gift card? All the money in your bank account? I would think of something.

"If you return to the pack house, you'll be going against our advice, and it will be difficult to guarantee your safety," Laramie spoke with vitriol.

"You couldn't guarantee anyone's safety anyway," Xan threw back.

"Okay," Agent Schaffer said, clearly trying to be the peace-maker. "If you are unwilling to go into the witness protection program, then I think the next best course of action would be to send one of our undercover agents to the pack estate. We could assign one of our deep cover agents to help monitor the property and ensure everyone's safety as much as possible."

Everyone sat silently for a minute, neither outright saying no nor enthusiastically agreeing either.

"Kai and I can move into the cabin when we get back, and whoever they send out can stay in my old room. Most of my stuff has been moved already, anyway, " I say.

The idea appealed to me, but Schaffer disagreed. He was hesitant about us distancing ourselves from the group while remaining on the pack's property.

With that idea dismissed, Kai suggested I move into her room since we should be living together, and all her belongings were still there. Then, whoever was sent out could stay in my room.

Neither Schaffer nor Laramie rejected the suggestion, so it was concluded.

Laramie excused herself to speak with the healer and told us the bureau would pay for the services since they were on the case trying to find Celeste. We didn't turn them down, so when that was settled, a plan of action was decided upon.

The agents wanted us to leave the area as soon as possible in case Celeste was still lingering, and we all agreed we were ready to go. They had a rental car they picked up from the airport when their plane landed, so they would escort us the rest of the way back to West Virginia.

When we got back on the road, it was around nine a.m. We were exhausted and ready to be home.

Several hours later, when we returned to the estate, the agents assumed guard positions around the property until the undercover agent arrived, which they said would be that evening.

Completely worn out, we all agreed to take a nap and reconvene in the late afternoon.

Twenty-Five

KAI

W hen I drift awake from my nap, I notice how utterly comfortable and warm I am. When I stretch my pointed toes, they graze flesh, and I become aware enough to realize why I'm so warm. A giant body is snuggled to me, wrapped around me like a koala.

It feels better than I imagined to be held like this. I sank closer into Alder's sleeping form.

When his hand came up to rub up and down my arm, I realized he wasn't actually asleep. I began to roll over to face him, but it turned out to be a painful experience since I had forgotten about the stitches on my shoulder.

He climbed out of bed and shuffled around to my other side, lying back down so I could see him. Scooting as close as he could, I rested my head against his shoulder.

The happiness I feel right now makes me question myself. Why did I wait so long to accept Alder as my mate? The day I met him, I knew almost immediately that he was meant to be mine, but I let history keep me from him.

Growing up, I witnessed the worst possible example of mates in my parents. Nothing was peaceful in our home. My mother manipulated and verbally abused my father, and I couldn't understand why they were together, or why my father was determined to stay with her.

Both my parents are long gone now, but I told myself long ago that if that was what mates were, I wanted no part of it. The trauma of my childhood made me rebel against the very idea of mates, choosing instead to focus on having a good time.

It wasn't until I saw how devoted Xan was to Finley and how he practically worships the ground she walks on that I began softening to the idea. Even so, I avoided Alder as if he had an incurable illness. Without Celeste trying to steal him, I don't know if I ever would have taken the leap to solidify our bond. What a tragedy that would have been.

Alder is a good male. He has shown me nothing but steadfast care since we met. I should have given him a chance sooner. I deeply regret how I've treated him.

Hugging him tightly, I whisper, "I'm so sorry."

He squeezes me back before pulling away to look at me. "You have nothing to be sorry for, little wolf."

I shake my head. "I do, though!" Now I'm sobbing uncontrollably.

"None of that," he tells me as he wipes tears off my face. When he has them all wiped away, he says, "Let's back up a little bit. What has you upset?"

I explain through more sobs, pouring my heart out. I tell him about my childhood, how awful my mother was to her 'mate'. I explain how scared I was to be trapped with someone and treated like my dad. I share my desire to never mate whether by fate or choice. Then, I express how guilty I feel for the way I've treated him, rebuffing his feelings and failing to give him a chance.

He listens without judgment. He doesn't interrupt me, patiently waiting until I've finished spilling my guts before speaking.

"See, there's nothing to apologize for. You and I are together; everything worked out exactly as it was meant to. Would it have been better if we hadn't had interference from Celeste? Yes, I wish we had never met her. But we ended up with the best possible outcome."

He comforts me until I finish crying before helping me sit up.

"Here," he says, handing me a glass of water.

"While you were still sleeping, I went and checked everything out. We still have an hour or more until everyone wants to meet to update the others. Drink this water to avoid dehydration."

I listen and sip it until the glass is empty.

His hand rubs small, comforting circles on my back. I return the glass to him, and he places it on the nightstand.

"Thank you."

"Are you hungry?" he asks.

Shaking my head, I reply, "Not yet. Maybe we can bring some snack items with us when we go to the meeting. The others might be hungry by then, too."

"I'll text Ry and see if he and Leora will put something together."

"Oh, don't bother them," I say.

"They won't mind. They understand we had a challenging time. They'll be glad to help "

"Fine," I agree.

He reaches back to the nightstand, but I cannot tell what he has picked up.

With a closed fist, he brings the object closer to me. He doesn't make eye contact when offering it to me.

A blush spreads across his cheeks, intense enough to be visible in the dim light of the room. "When I checked the time we needed to be ready for the meeting, Finley mentioned you might want this."

I finally catch a glimpse of it: it's a vial of the monthly birth control potion that Xan brews for Finley.

The embarrassment on his face is priceless, with his hand gripping the back of his neck as he speaks.

"Um, apparently she could tell what we were up to before the fight." He taps his nose, indicating that she could smell it.

I can't help but cackle at how difficult this conversation seems for him to endure. My heart feels like it's doing loop-de-loops in my chest, zooming with joy as I watch him stumble through it.

"We never discussed that, and since my squatch was mostly in control until we were together, it wasn't quite on my mind. I'm sorry. I should have been more in control and asked you before we, you know. So anyway, she sent this in case you want it."

I return it to him.

"I don't actually need this."

When he looks at me for further explanation, I admit that I've already started taking it once a month. I just never told Finley, but I appreciated that she had my back.

Hoping to change the subject, knowing how flustered this one has made my poor giant, I decide it's best to get cleaned up.

Even covered in blood after our battle, I still smelled of sex. A few months ago, I would have felt embarrassed by it, but as a mated woman, I now feel a sense of smug satisfaction about carrying Alder's scent. However, out of consideration for my friends' sensitive noses, I will take a shower.

When I try to get up, Alder protests heavily. He's so worried about my well-being that it's cute, although unnecessary. I'm injured, but not a fragile piece of glass.

I try to protest when he scoops me into his arms, insisting on helping me shower. When it seems my efforts are ineffective, I relax back into his warmth.

"Enough, little wolf. I'm going to take care of you," he said in what was probably the gruffest voice I'd ever heard Alder use. It resonated with authority, so opposite of the giant teddy bear vibes he usually gives off.

I might be a strong, independent wolf who can fiercely take down men twice my size in a fight, but the tone he used is doing things for me.

He helps me clean up, taking extra care with my wound and avoiding soaking my stitches. He also tenderly washes my hair. When I get out, he doesn't even let me dry myself; instead, he wraps me in a fluffy towel and does it himself.

The luxury treatment he's giving me makes me feel inexplicably turned on. When he lays me down on the bed and attempts to get clothes to dress me, I can't help but pout.

"You've created a problem, and I'm not in a position to address it."

When he turns back to see what I'm referring to, I spread my legs slightly, allowing him to see my wet center.

A subtle smirk appears on his face as he prowls back to me.

"Are you feeling needy, little wolf?"

In response, I spread my legs wider and give him the most pitiful expression I can muster.

When he gets close enough, I try to pull him to me. Injury be damned, I desire this man. His body against mine. I want him, need him.

Memories flood in from the other night, recalling all the things he did to me and the way he made my body feel.

I complain in earnest when he prevents me from climbing him like a fucking tree.

"This isn't how it's going to go," he tells me in that gruff voice again. "Lie back."

I want to protest, but I'm too freaking turned on to do anything except listen.

"You're such a good girl."

Oh, fates, why did that make me moan? I've never had a praise kink. This feels like uncharted territory as I sense myself getting wetter between my thighs.

He whispers everything he desires to do to me when I'm better, layering my skin with kisses between his dirty, highly detailed words.

When it starts to feel like I'm going to combust, I finally feel him settle between my spread thighs. Hooking his hands under my legs, he gently yet firmly drags me closer to him.

His mouth finds my core and he teases my clit with his tongue. His short beard grazes my soft skin, the friction driving me wild. He's playing games with me. It's the only way to describe how he builds me up and then slows down his pace. Not quite allowing me to find relief from my deep-seated need.

A soft growl escapes me between moans of pleasure.

"Stop teasing me," I snap.

He laughs against my sensitive skin, the vibrations creating a new high.

"Fine, fucking come," he says before he attacks my core with even greater enthusiasm. The slick noises coming from our joining are downright indecent, and I find myself following his instructions. Euphoria floods my body; my soul leaves this realm behind before bringing me back to earth.

He gently brings me back down as my orgasm fades.

When he helps me sit up, I grab the collar of his shirt, pulling him to me with the fabric. My lips meet his in an open-mouthed kiss as I chase the taste of myself on his tongue.

When we break apart, I explicitly detail what I plan to do to him when my arm is healed.

He helped me put on a pair of leggings and an oversized T-shirt that was loose against my pained shoulder. He was just getting the hem settled when there was a loud bang on our door.

The rude knocking is followed by, "Quit fucking around and get out here."

I recognize Callum's voice and start to wonder why I have been tolerating him recently. I might need to reassess my acceptance of him.

ALDER

We reluctantly head to the study for the family meeting. We are the last to arrive; Ry and Leora are just placing a snack tray down, and there is a cooler of drinks by the coffee table.

We settle onto one of the couches. I can't find the strength to release my hold on Kai, positioning myself close to her. Logically, I know she's fine, but the entire ordeal has taken a toll on my nerves.

I assemble a plateful of fruit and other items before thrusting it at Kai. When she doesn't immediately take it, my insides start to get itchy. When we get back, she hasn't eaten, and my squatch demands that we take care of her.

Noticing her hesitation, I pick up a strawberry and attempt to hand-feed her.

An amused laugh escapes Hadeon, which is strikingly out of character for the stoic vampire.

Finley assesses me and once she confirms my beast is riding me hard to take care of my mate she starts the meeting.

"Right, let's disregard that." She gestures at me. "We need to discuss what happened."

With his arms crossed and a scowl on his face, Hadeon asks, "Yes. Who wants to explain why we have two agents from the International Bureau of Magical Enforcement on our property?"

We recount everything that happened while we were in Kentucky, including the ambush and Celeste's reappearance. When we tell them about Kai's injury, Leora gasps and requests reassurance that she's okay.

Hadeon is across the room in the blink of an eye thanks to his vampiric speed. He wants to examine the wound, and my mate obliges him. I can't lie; it makes me uncomfortable that he is getting so close and personal with it. When his face nears her shoulder, I growl from deep in my chest.

If he tries to bite my mate, I don't care about our strength difference; I'll kick his ass.

Rather than engaging in any untoward behavior, he simply smells it. Everyone around us scrunches their noses in either disgust or confusion.

He strides back across the room as if nothing had happened, simply stating, "The healer did a nice job. There's no sign of infection."

Huh, I didn't know vampires could detect things like that by smell. While I'm relieved to find out it's not infected, I still feel like it was a strange move.

He leaves the room for a minute before returning, sipping from a blood bag. Did the scent of my woman make him hungry? That son of a bitch.

I glare at him while he slurps from the straw protruding from the plastic.

Seeming to sense the tension in the room, Leora jumps up with a beaming smile and proclaims that everyone needs a little joy as she spreads some of her magic around the room. One of her powers as a light fairy is to influence feelings—specifically, she can help settle unease and create feelings of joy.

Once everyone is a bit less tense, Finley explains the ultimatum that Agent Schaffer offered: witness protection or an undercover agent staying here.

"The agent they're sending will arrive tonight," I add.

Hadeon uses the projector to display several camera feeds that he installed when Xan called from the healer's cottage. He shows a view with at least a dozen feeds. I'm not sure how he manages to monitor so many at once, but he assures us that he can.

The group is arguing about different protocols to establish for our protection here at the property when the doorbell rings.

Hadeon uses an app on his phone to identify who is at the door. Since it is the agents, he invites them in and directs them to the study.

When they enter the room, it isn't just Agents Schaffer and Laramie. An unfamiliar woman stands with them. She's probably about five and a half feet tall with a slim, muscular build. Her straight black hair falls to about shoulder length. She has warm brown skin and dark eyes that are almost black. When she makes eye contact with me, I sense something that fills me with wariness. Her pitch-colored eyes seem to swirl. She stares at me as if she is examining my soul, which is a very nerve-wracking experience, to be sure. Before she looks away, a sparkle appears in her irises, almost like the twinkling of stars.

She finally looks away, and I wonder if that felt as long and intrusive to everyone else as it did to me.

Agent Schaffer clears his throat before introducing her, saying, "This is Laila Aziz. She's the agent who will be responsible for your protection detail."

Hadeon scowls slightly as he looks her over. I haven't known him to be outright rude, so I'm unsure what his issue is.

But then he speaks, "Honestly, this isn't really necessary. And not to be mean or anything, but she's kind of small; I'm not sure how much help she would be if we are under attack again."

Schaffer's grin appears positively feral as he states, "You'd be surprised, actually. Agent Aziz is one of our top assets."

Laughter trails behind Schaffer and Laramie as they exit, leaving our safety in the hands of this unknown agent.

Twenty-Seven

CELESTE

Things took an unfortunate turn. All these weeks spent infiltrating the Harrison pack, another wasted love potion, and weeks of planning- all for nought.

It was easy to slip Riggs the potion, and it worked too well. The alpha was head over tail for me. Little good it does now.

What does a girl have to do to get a competent henchman?

I chose the Harrison pack because of the tight fist with which Riggs ruled them. His subordinates were meant to be easily persuaded, so I didn't anticipate an uprising.

When that furry golden wolf charged into the fight with his band of usurpers, I hoped they would be defeated swiftly. However, when my infuriating cousin and his friends escaped, I realized I might have chosen the wrong male to beguile.

It became clear that the fight was lost, so I fled.

Running toward the creek, I drenched my clothes in the frigid water, hoping it would wash away some of my scent and make me harder to track.

It took a while, but eventually, I reached a highway. Because of the early hour, there weren't many cars yet. When I saw a car coming, I rushed to the edge of the road, holding my arm at a weird angle. I pretended to be injured.

When the car I flagged down stopped, it was all too easy to subdue the driver and steal his vehicle.

Humans can be rather foolish and easily deceived.

I didn't have a destination in mind yet, but I floored the gas pedal knowing I needed to leave the location as quickly as possible. As I drove, I resolved that while I was momentarily defeated, this would not be the end.

This might have started when I tried to take that squatch, but things have escalated. I don't care about that anymore; it was a matter of principle.

I imagine it would hurt very much to lose a mate. Maybe I'd put capturing the squatch on the back burner for now; instead, I would focus on getting rid of his wolf mate. She has been a thorn in my side, foiling my plans for far too long.

Twenty-Eight

ALDER

Last night, after we introduced Agent Aziz, she quickly excused herself to do a perimeter check. Everyone who went on the trip to the Harrison Pack meeting was still exhausted despite our daytime naps. We broke up for the night and all went off to get some extra rest—or at least that was the plan.

I followed Kai back to her room—our room now. We should have been resting, but as soon as I closed the door behind us, Kai was on me. Knowing she was injured, I did my best to deflect her advances—I truly tried—even if it left me throbbing with need.

She was undeterred by my reminders of her injured shoulder or our need for rest. She was just as insatiable as during our previous times together.

I surrendered to her desire, and we spent hours giving each other indescribable pleasure.

When she won me over, one of our compromises was that we had to be gentle.

She lay on her side, her good shoulder resting on the mattress as I spooned her, fucking her from behind.

No matter how many times she begged for me to go faster or harder, I set a slow pace of deep thrusts. She protested, saying to stop trying to make love to her. But would it really be so bad if we loved each other? I asked her that exact question, and her answer hurt more than I thought possible. Yes, she said, it would be detrimental.

After that round, we were both exhausted and fell asleep while I remained nestled in her heat.

This morning, when I woke up beside her, I wasn't quite ready to face her in the light of day, knowing she would be able to see the devastation on my face.

When we first met, it was obvious that Kai didn't just dislike me—she hated my guts. I hadn't done anything to earn that sort of treatment from her, but I tried my best to win her over.

Kai interrupting that sham mating ceremony while I was under the thrall of Celeste's love potion made me believe that she had developed feelings for me. When she bit me, bonding herself to me, I thought surely she accepted me.

Our newly developed sexual experiences truly made me believe we were on the right path to a beautiful future, until her words last night bludgeoned my heart, crumbling my hopes and leaving me only rubble behind.

Before leaving her room, I left a note on my pillow, letting her know I didn't want to wake her and that I had some things to do today.

All day, I invented tasks to keep myself busy, doing my best to avoid interacting with anyone. By nightfall, I had successfully evaded Kai and barely engaged in small talk with my friends.

The downside of all the quiet was the space it left for persistent thoughts to trouble me.

Most squatches lead solitary lives in the wilderness, choosing to live only with their mate and offspring—who typically go off on their own upon reaching maturity.

Growing up as an only child would have been enough to make me lonely, but the isolation of living off the grid intensified that feeling. My parents were great parents, but sometimes, I felt like an outsider. They were the type of mates who were so disgustingly in love that I felt like a useless third wheel most of the time.

When I was a child, I would fall asleep in the cabin loft, dreaming of being surrounded by people who loved me. As I grew, my longing for that closeness only intensified. Though my parents loved me, they didn't understand me. They perceived my craving for companionship as a flaw, as if something were wrong with me. This perception made the wedge between us feel even larger.

When I turned eighteen, they "helped" me pack my belongings. They attempted to be gentle while pushing me out of their metaphorical nest, but it didn't lessen my sense of betrayal.

They said it was my time to forge my own destiny. To build my own home somewhere, find a squatch to mate with, and have children of my own.

Nothing about their plan sounded appealing to me. I was already painfully lonely, and they wanted me to venture off on my own. They expected me to find a nice squatch, but given that it is an endangered species, that was an unlikely undertaking. On top of all that, they wanted me to procreate—why would I want to do that if this was the treatment they expected me to give my future child? I would never treat my flesh and blood that way.

When they gave me money to start my life, I left and never looked back.

It was expected that I stay isolated as a squatch normally would, but screw that. If I controlled my future, with no one influencing my choices, I decided I'd create a future of my own making.

With just a backpack of clothes and the few thousand dollars my parents gave me, I left the wild.

Once I emerged from the forest, I walked along an unfamiliar highway. I wasn't sure where I was or what my destination was, but I was confident I would recognize it when I found it.

Hours of walking had tired me out, so I rested on the side of the road when I saw a car approaching.

I'd never seen a car before, but I knew what they looked like from one of the schoolbooks my mom taught me from.

The older man driving noticed me sitting on my backpack. He asked what a kid like me was doing out in the middle of nowhere. When I gave a vague answer about traveling, he seemed to take pity on me and offered me a ride to town.

He talked my ear off during the drive, but thankfully he didn't pry too much into my personal life, which I appreciated. I would have needed to lie, and that would have made me feel guilty after he was so kind to me. We rode together for about an hour before reaching a small town.

When we went our separate ways, I made sure to thank him for his kindness, and he wished me luck on my trip. The generosity of a complete stranger warmed my heart and made me feel braver about venturing into the unknown.

There was a 50s-themed diner in that town, and I chose to make it my first destination because I had developed quite an appetite.

I was unfamiliar with the menu items, so I ordered four different meals to try them all. The waitress was surprised by my request but brought the meals without comment.

Every new thing I tried was better than the last. I was amazed that humans could access this type of food whenever they wanted. What a fantastic way to live! I decided right then that I would continue to explore all kinds of human cuisine.

When I was full and unable to eat another bite, I sat back in the red pleather booth and contemplated my next move. I relied on my instincts to guide me to where I belonged. This town was nice, but it didn't feel like the right one.

I had been lost in thought when a dark-haired stranger slid into the seat opposite me. He wore a black leather jacket over a plain black shirt. He seemed nonthreatening, yet there was something about him that felt sly.

Having never met a warlock, I didn't know what type of supernatural being he was, only that he was one; you could feel the tingle of magic in the air surrounding him.

He was not offended when I asked him what he was, though he told me some might take offense to outright asking. He told me he had a feeling we were supposed to meet, about the town he was from, and about the nightclub he owned, where all species of supernaturals were welcome.

When he invited me to go with him, it all seemed too good to be true. When I realized he seemed genuine, I decided to see what happened. If it didn't pan out, no harm, no foul; it wasn't like I had a plan anyway.

All these years later, I could confirm that I was meant to be here. Xan brought me to West Virginia and made me part of his friend group. Back then, it was just Hadeon and Ry—until Ry found his mate Leora. Eventually, Xan found Finley, and there was the chaos with Fallon—the previous Fang alpha—which brought all kinds of new people into our lives, including my mate.

Still feeling a bit too sensitive about our conversation, I decided to try sleeping on the couch now that everyone had returned to their rooms for the night.

I lay down on the living room couch, which had a nice velvety texture. It was enjoyable to rub my palms against it and feel how smooth it was. However, whoever designed this piece of furniture didn't have someone of my size in mind when creating it. I was much longer than the couch. When I lay on my back, my chest touched both edges of the cushion, barely fitting, while my legs extended off the end by a couple of feet.

Despite my discomfort, I closed my eyes, intent on getting some sleep. I almost reached dreamland when footsteps alerted me that I was no longer alone. When I opened my eyes to see who had entered the room, I was met with the glare of the person I had been avoiding all day. The look she gave me could have skewered lesser men.

Twenty-Nine

KAI

When I woke that morning to find a note from Alder saying he was up getting some things done, I thought nothing of it. I had things to handle from when we were away, so I got ready for the day and headed out to make some rounds.

A couple of hours later, I began to sense that something wasn't quite right. Ever since Alder and I accepted our mating bonds, he had stayed close to me, stopping by to chat or at least being near me while I worked. But today, he was nowhere to be seen.

When I mentioned not seeing him, I received different answers about his whereabouts. Xan told me that Al was helping move some boxes to storage. Hadeon told me that Al was on a grocery run the last he knew, but Laila was on the premises, so he must be here somewhere since he is supposed to have a bodyguard.

It was weird, but I didn't dwell on it, moving on to handle more of the tasks that needed my attention today. But at family dinner, Alder wasn't present. Dinner is his favorite meal of the day, and he loves being surrounded by all his favorite people. This is when I started to worry.

Callum mentioned receiving a text from Alder informing him that he wouldn't be here for dinner. I knew they were starting to become closer friends than when Callum first joined us, but did he hold a higher rank than me on his contact list? Even entertaining that thought made my wolf's hackles rise, even though it was silly. Perhaps I should make him disappear.

By night, when I still hadn't seen him and went to lie down, only to find him absent, I was pissed.

Was he hiding from me? Did he change his mind about us?

I had already changed into a nightgown for the evening, but I didn't let that stop me from searching for my errant mate. If anyone had a problem seeing me this way, they could stuff it.

Contemplating the disappearing act intensified my anger as I marched down the stairs, tracking a scent trail.

I followed his smell until it became heavily concentrated, letting me know it was fresh. I stopped at the door blocking off the living room. The door wasn't shut completely, and I saw him through the crack. He was lying on the couch, which was far too small, his legs hanging off the end. It looked highly uncomfortable. Why was he down here?

The door creaked as I pushed it open. Upon stepping into the room, he shot up from the couch with a stunned expression.

He looked either nervous or guilty, but I wasn't sure why. I gestured toward him as I asked, "What are you doing?"

"Just resting," he answered, laying back down. With his arms crossed over his chest, he appeared emotionally closed off as I stood there watching him.

"I understand that. But that can't be comfortable. Come to bed," I said, extending my hand towards him.

When he didn't take it, my stomach felt like it dropped to the floor. My heart raced, and even though I had never experienced a panic attack before, I felt like I was dangerously close to having one.

He had changed his mind. He didn't want me. He was rejecting me. What would happen to us since we were bonded?

My thoughts raced when he said again, "I figured I'd sleep here for the night." He acted as if none of this was a big deal or out of character, completely nonchalant. He's only ever been the opposite, chalant. Damn, that isn't even a word, but if it were, that's what would describe his usual behavior.

I wanted to say, "Don't be silly," and I wanted to suggest that his place was with me, but I couldn't express any of those thoughts. My chest felt too tight and painful.

What emerged was a growl from my wolf. She didn't appreciate feeling betrayed, not by anyone, but especially not by him.

"Why?" I asked when I regained control of my wolf. If it were up to her, we would act now and ask questions later. This wasn't the time to let her take over; Alder is sensitive, and this situation would require finesse and care.

He didn't respond at first but gave me a deadpan look. What happened?

"I thought it might be best for both of us if I stayed here for now."

Sweat began to trickle down my neck, and I felt dizzy. I believed things were going well, that we were making progress in getting to know each other.

My eyes stung, but I tried to suppress it. Keeping my voice as steady as possible, I said, "I don't understand."

"You were clear about what you want and don't want last night. You don't want us to be in love. How am I supposed to be around you all the time while keeping my feelings at bay? I'm doing my best to follow your wishes, but that means I also need to protect myself. I can't sleep beside you, share intimate moments, or be close to you if you don't want me and can't see yourself loving me back." His voice cracked while he spoke, intensifying the pain within me.

Panic is the only feeling I have at this moment. He's leaving. He doesn't want me. I just began to embrace the idea and started diving in, but he is giving up on me.

"That's not what I want—" I begin, but he interrupts me.

"I can't." His eyes are so sad. It feels like a sledgehammer to my gut.

"Please," I whisper softly.

"You don't want love between us, and I could wait if it were a matter of timing, but I don't think I could stay in limbo, only to fall deeper in love with you, only to be rejected." He sighed.

"I can't." His eyes were full of tears as he rubbed his chest. I wondered if he felt the physical ache there, just like I did.

He loves me. He has mentioned it twice in the last few minutes indirectly. He doesn't truly want this to end. He wants me to love him in return. Right now, I need to be courageous. Can I be brave if it means saving him from pain?

He starts to stand up and walk away, not even glancing back at me. When he reaches the door on the other side of the room, I yell, "Wait."

He pauses at the threshold but doesn't turn back.

"I was scared," I admit.

Thirty

ALDER

I stood completely still at her confession. Her voice resonated with sincerity, but it was difficult to envision my strong and fierce mate fearing anything. When I turned back to face her, she had moved to stand in front of me.

Her blue eyes shone suspiciously as if they were brimming with tears, but that couldn't be true. She always barricaded her emotions behind a brick wall. She wasn't truly about to cry, was she?

She grabbed my large hand in one of her smaller hands and gripped it tight. Looking me directly in the eyes, she said, "I'm sorry."

The bruised feeling in my heart felt less intense, but did that mean she was willing to be in this with me? Or did she just feel bad for hurting me?

Kai gently tugged me behind her as she made her way to the couch and sat down. She encouraged me to sit next to her, but the effort behind the tug was soft enough to indicate that she was leaving me the choice to follow or not.

I chose to sit.

"My parents were fate blessed mates too."

The tone of voice conflicted with the statement. What should have been a happy thing sounded sad when it came from her lips. I wasn't sure what to say, but thankfully she spoke again before I had to figure it out.

"I'm sure you've heard talk about how I've always avoided emotional attachments and have little interest in relationships." She briefly paused until I nodded. I had heard that, but I wasn't sure what the driving force behind it was. "My parents were so toxic together. Growing up, I saw the way their relationship was and thought, if this is how fate deals the cards, I want no part of it. My mother was manipulative and cruel to my father. Nothing he did was ever enough. She always found something to belittle him about. And he didn't do anything to stop it. He didn't stand up for himself. He just let it happen because she was his mate, and he didn't want to live without her, even if it would have been a better life for him."

She was clearly crying now, sniffling as she finished telling me about her parents. We had started this conversation on what felt like opposite sides of a battlefield. However, if we wanted to win the war instead of self-sabotaging, we needed to be on the same side. I would cross the metaphorical line to her side if she would stand beside me.

I couldn't bear to see her hurt and know that there was nothing I could do to fix it. The damage was in the past; long gone history. The only thing I could do now was support her and show her something different.

When I pulled her body close, she came willingly. With her head resting on my shoulder, I held her tightly. We would not become them. I would rather die than cause her an ounce pain.

I gently raised her face to mine so that she could see into my eyes when I spoke.

"That will never be us," I infused as much confidence and strength as I could into my voice. "I want to spend the rest of my life loving you. I would never treat you that way."

Her eyes darted away from mine, as if uncertain, so I continued speaking.

"I might not be perfect. I'm going to mess up sometimes, but it will never be intentional. We will face everything together. From the moment you bit me, we became a team. If we believe in our team, we'll do life together. Imagine the most beautiful future you can think of, tell me what it looks like, and I'll give it to you."

Her shoulders, previously raised to her ears during our conversation, gradually relaxed as she lowered her guard.

She hugged me tightly and murmured her agreement. We were determined to give this our all. We were going to be okay—more than okay.

Thirty-One

CELESTE

Hiding out in an abandoned building wasn't the plan, but so far, nothing had gone right. I was on the run from the International Bureau of Magical Enforcement, my cousin's stupid group of miscreants, and now, thanks to Riggs, I was also being hunted by the Harrison pack.

I'd been hiding in this building for a few days, and I was already done sitting around in the dark, with a dank smell irritating my nose.

I'd stolen one of those battery-powered camping lanterns from a store nearby, and as I paced, it was the only light in the room. With each step, my feet hit the concrete harder.

When I tried to push my hair away from my face, my hand got stuck in the strands. My normally blue locks were almost black due to the caked-on gunk from my sprint through the woods and my inability to wash them.

This was not how any of this was meant to unfold. Everything I aimed to accomplish was beginning to feel hopeless. I was teetering on the edge of my rope. But if I was going down, I resolved to take them down with me.

My pacing was interrupted by a scraping noise coming from the boarded-up door I had smashed in when I arrived.

There weren't many potions left in my arsenal, and my supplies were running low. I needed to restock soon, but for now, I grabbed one I knew would temporarily stun an attacker and crept down the stairs.

When I reached the bottom of the stairs, the figure standing in front of me was shocking. Riggs stood in the doorway, the light streaming in behind him illuminating him in grim detail.

He had cuts and what I assumed were bites all over his body. Dried blood and mysterious substances surrounded him wherever I looked.

"Did you miss me?" he asked in a voice that I had never heard sound so cold.

I was seen as downright evil, and even the sound of his voice sent a shiver of fear through me. He seemed half feral. His presence felt dangerous.

With my most convincing fake smile, I said, "Of course."

I walked toward him, keeping the potion tightly wrapped in my fist and hidden behind my back, just in case.

"They will pay for everything they have done." The gleam in his eyes was pure malice.

"We will ensure they do," I replied.

I was no longer alone, and together we would take down everyone who had wronged us.

Thirty-Two

KAI

We had been back at our pack house for a few days, and so far, nothing has happened. It has been business as usual. We have all been getting back into our pre-Celeste routines.

This morning, Agent Aziz escorted Alder to a meeting out of town. The rest of us wanted to accompany them, but Agent Aziz forbade it. She mentioned that the property was likely under surveillance and that bringing a large group could make us a target. Personally, I believed that having more people would provide more protection, but I wasn't in charge. We reluctantly agreed to stay behind.

Finley had a list of tasks for me to assist with today, so I worked my way through the tasks, trying to keep busy.

There was only one item left to tackle, but before I could start, I received a phone call. One of our pack members had been asked to help patrol the property while Aziz was gone.

I knew that if he was calling me, something had come up, so I braced myself before answering, "This is Kai."

"It's Tyler. I was on the northwest side of the property and found some wolf prints. It might be nothing, but it doesn't smell like one of ours—none that I recognize, anyway."

He is a newer pack member, so he doesn't know all the members yet, but we are limiting the number of visitors to the property until everything blows over. It would be better to check it out.

"Send me your location, and I'll meet you."

After disconnecting the call with Tyler, I immediately called Ry.

"Hey, I'm making lunch for everyone. What kind of sandwich do you—" I interrupted him before he could finish.

"There might be someone here who shouldn't be. It could be nothing, but I'm going to check it out. Tell Leora to keep Finley busy; there's no need to worry her before we know anything. I'll forward the location to Hadeon when I get it, have him come meet me there, and lock down the house, just in case."

He agreed, and I ended the call.

When the message arrived from Tyler, I dashed into the woods in my wolf form.

On four legs, I sprinted, weaving between trees. The wind felt amazing as it caressed my fur. It had recently rained, so the white on my paws started to become muddy as I got further from the house.

Occasionally, I'd stop to sniff the breeze, ensuring there were no unfamiliar scents. So far, the only thing I'd picked up was Tyler.

When I reached the spot where I was to meet him, I skidded to a halt. It had been less than ten minutes, but I hadn't seen him anywhere.

Cautiously, I explored, searching for where he had gone, but it didn't take long before I found his body lying on the ground.

It was hard to see if he was breathing, so I had to get closer to check. I gave a cursory look around but didn't see anyone else.

When I stood over him, I could see his chest rising and falling, but it was slight. This close, I could smell the iron tang of blood. As I looked him over, I noticed a bit of it pooling beneath his head.

I shifted back to my human form and turned his head to look. The blood appeared excessive for the gash on the back of his head, but I knew that sometimes head wounds could be quite bloody.

Deciding that he was merely unconscious and not in mortal peril, I attempted to wake him. At first, I shook his shoulder gently, but when that didn't work, I became more impatient. I needed to know what caused his injury quickly; we could be in trouble without even realizing it.

As I glanced over my shoulder, I still didn't see anyone, but I wanted to move this along.

Gently slapping his cheek, I tried again to rouse him. I'd apologize later, but we couldn't sit here like prey.

I was just about to try again when I heard the snap of a twig. Instantly, I was on my feet, alert.

When I turned toward the sound, I found Celeste standing in the clearing. She looked terrible. The clothes she wore were dirty, her skin paler than I'd ever seen it, and her hair was a knotted mess. It seemed like she'd been living in the woods. I almost felt sympathy for her, but that feeling didn't last long when I remembered everything she had done.

It was likely the wrong thing to do, but I couldn't resist goading her, saying, "You look lovely."

"So original," she scoffed.

"Why did you knock Tyler out? That wasn't very nice." She was unpredictable, and I thought that verbally sparring with her might occupy her for a moment while I figured out what to do.

"Oh, that wasn't me." She smiled in a way that could only be described as malevolently triumphant.

She wasn't alone; that much became clear when a noise came from behind me.

Shit. Why didn't I smell either of them? I had specifically been searching for scents.

Knowing the threat she posed, I knew better than to turn my back on her, so I simply turned my head. With a quick glance over my shoulder, I saw a large wolf.

I angled my body and took a couple of discreet steps back. I needed to keep an eye on both since I was outnumbered, as Tyler was still lying on the ground

The wolf was Riggs. I thought he would be long dead after the uprising from his pack. Unfortunately, for me, that wasn't the case. He stood growling in front of me. His fur was matted, with many patches missing in places. The feral energy radiating from him made him my greatest potential threat. It was unlikely to rationalize with him; he would be out for blood.

Hadeon hadn't made it here yet, but I needed to warn the others. I took my phone out of my pocket and dialed his number before putting it back in. Hopefully, he'd answer and be able to hear what was happening.

Perhaps I could postpone whatever they have planned until Hadeon arrives. That seems to be my best option at the moment.

"I imagine you'll be disappointed to hear this, but Alder isn't here right now. You've made a wasted trip."

Celeste's face lit up with glee as she said, "Oh, we're not here for him." She waved away the idea. "We're here for you."

Then Riggs started to approach me, taking one fierce step at a time, with saliva dripping from his bared teeth.

Seeing I was out of time, I sprinted away from them as fast as I could. Remembering the call, I stayed in my human form, hoping Hadeon was listening.

Sadly, it was Riggs who reached me first. Searing pain shot through my body as his jaw clamped down on my ankle, pulling me down.

A moment later, everything went black.

Thirty-Three

ALDER

This had to be one of the most awkward road trips I've ever experienced, not that I've had many. But this was genuinely uncomfortable. There has only been an exchange of a few words throughout the entire time.

We left the house a few hours ago when Agent Aziz received a message stating that we were needed. Being separated from Kai didn't feel right to me, but at this moment, there wasn't much I could do. I would attend this meeting, answer any questions they might have, and hope to return home as quickly as we could.

Turning the corner, the vehicle started descending, driving into what looked to be an underground parking garage. I've only seen parking garages go up, never down. I was curious about how many levels it had, but more than that, the fact that we were going underground with so much concrete above us made me feel claustrophobic.

We were stopped by a guard who scanned the badge that Agent Aziz presented. After we were cleared for entry, we quickly located a parking spot.

I followed as I was led to an elevator. I was curious about many things, but for now, I kept them to myself. Maybe I could ask them on the way home. If there was something to talk about, it would be less awkward, hopefully.

A man at the reception desk checked us in before calling Agent Schaffer to let him know we were there.

"Yes, sir." The man furrowed his eyebrows as he spoke on the phone.

We sat waiting for permission to be sent back. At least, the seats in the lounge area were much more comfortable than those in the car. It was a much-needed relief for my aching back, which had felt scrunched up for too long in the car. The car we rode in was too small to be comfortable for someone of my size, as my legs were cramped for the entire trip.

Ten minutes of sitting in silence passed before we were addressed. I expected the receptionist to lead us back to see Agent Schaffer, but instead, he marched out from one of the hallways.

He stood before us in a suit, looking much more put together than the last time I saw him. He grimaced as he asked, "What are you doing here?"

Agent Aziz looked back at him, confused. "We came here after receiving your message."

Schaffer's face went pale before he said, "I didn't send a message."

I jumped to my feet, and fear started to race through my body. We had been told to come here, but the message wasn't really sent from Schaffer. The ruse had brought us here, and we had come alone, leaving the pack unprotected.

Ringing came from Schaffer's pocket as he pulled out his phone. He asked us to stay here for a minute while he figured out what was happening, but my instincts urged me that we needed to get home.

Schaffer wasn't gone long, and when he returned, he said, "I'm sorry, but this is necessary," before raising what appeared to be a gun toward me. I froze in surprise as he pulled the trigger, but instead of a bullet, a dart struck my neck.

"Ah," I yelped. That stung. "What was that?"

He didn't answer me; instead, he told Aziz to catch me. I didn't understand why he said that since I was fine, and even if I weren't, I didn't believe she'd be able to lift me because of our size difference.

When she stood beside me, I began to feel sleepy.

"What was th—" I attempted to ask, but my words slurred as I fell, landing in a pair of slender arms.

HADEON

When Ry attempted to distract everyone, I sensed that something was happening, though I wasn't sure what. Then he informed me that Kai needed help. I readied myself as quickly as I could to assist her, only pausing long enough to tell the others to lock the doors on my way out.

Kai called, and I stopped to answer, hoping she was calling to say it was a false alarm or that the problem had been handled.

Optimism isn't my thing; I tend to stick closely to realism, so I shouldn't have been disappointed when I answered only to find out that nothing had been handled.

With one hand, I held the device to my ear as I once again continued on the path to Kai's location.

The sound wasn't great, leading me to assume Kai wasn't holding the phone close to her. It was smart of her to call, even if she couldn't speak to me this way, I could hear, and from the sounds of things, Celeste was here.

Holding the phone was slowing me down, so I stopped for a second to turn on a recording app to save the call audio. Then, I put the phone back in my pocket and ran as fast as I could.

When I reached my destination, I had to double-check the coordinates because no one was there. Then, I heard a grunt coming from a nearby bush.

I maintained my guard as I approached it, uncertain of what I would discover.

As I pulled back a branch to get a better look, I found Tyler. He was struggling, so I helped him sit up and move away from the bush. Once he was in the open, I could see the bloody gash on his head.

The only person I could scent in the area besides Kai was Tyler, and the only blood belonged to him, so hopefully that meant Kai was okay.

"What happened?" I asked him while keeping my head on a swivel, looking for potential threats.

"I was on patrol and spotted some tracks." He pointed to where he found them. "It was strange because they looked fresh, but I couldn't smell anything. I called Kai to inform her while I searched for the trespassers. I had just sent Kai a text with the coordinates when something hit me in the head. I was knocked out, and I only regained consciousness when they were dragging Kai away. When she saw me trying to get up, she mouthed 'fake it,' so I did. I pretended to still be unconscious, and they left, but

I must have been in and out of consciousness because I don't remember getting into the bushes.

I sensed that I already knew the answer, but I still asked, "Who took her?"

"There were two of them: one human and a wolf. I've never seen them before, so I don't know who they are. The human was a petite woman with blue hair. She was dressed like a character from a sitcom, but looked so bedraggled that she could have passed for an extra in a zombie movie. The wolf was large and had black fur, but it was damaged. He had bites and missing hair everywhere. It looks like he climbed his way out of hell."

I knew for certain that the woman was Celeste, but I was less certain about the wolf. I would need to speak with the agent on the case.

Before helping Tyler back to the house, I searched for any trails left behind by Kai or her abductors, but I only found a couple of drag marks leading away. It wasn't the ideal way to start looking for her.

Removing my phone from my pocket, I called Leora, who would arrange for a doctor to examine Tyler. Given his head injury and the fact that he had been knocked unconscious, I was concerned about the possibility of a concussion. She assured me that she would call the doctor before I hung up and then called Agent Schaffer.

"We have a huge problem."

Thirty-Five

ALDER

The first thing I noticed when I woke up was the bright fluorescent lights that burned my retinas. As I lay there, I wondered where I was, and then I realized I was on what appeared to be a medical examination table. I attempted to sit up, but I found myself restrained by thick leather straps buckled around my body every few feet.

The sight of my body being held down made me panic, and I thrashed around, trying to escape to no avail. My attempts to get free were loud, as I wasn't in the right frame of mind to be sneaky. After a few clangs of the straps and thumps of my feet hitting the metal side, the door opened.

"Good, you're awake," Agent Schaffer said as he entered, closely followed by a nervous-looking Laramie and a guilt-ridden Aziz.

Fuming over the lingering betrayal, I growled, "What's the meaning of this? Let me go!"

Schaffer looked chagrined but shook his head and replied, "I'm sorry, but this is for everyone's protection—including your own. We have some news that might be upsetting, and I decided it would be best to keep you contained until you've processed it."

Now I was even more confused. He invited us to come here, then seemed surprised to see us. Now he's acting as if someone has died, and I'm going to destroy everything in sight. Wait— "Is someone dead?"

He exhaled, "Goodness no. Not so severe, but still not great. There's no easy way to say this, so I'm just going to rip the band-aid off. The message agent Aziz received instructing her to bring you here was a ruse. You two came here, leaving the pack compound less protected. Your friend Hadeon called me; Celeste made her next move."

Schaffer was withholding information, which stressed me out more than waking up tied up.

"What happened?" I gritted out.

"Celeste and an accomplice, likely Riggs Harrison if our intelligence is accurate, arrived at the pack property. They managed to incapacitate a wolf named Tyler who was on patrol." He sighed deeply. "They abducted your mate, Kai."

My efforts to escape the grips of this damn table intensified. My inner squatch roared in frustration when we failed.

Our mate was somewhere out there with the enemy. It was a torturous thought. Even worse was the idea: what if she isn't?

Maybe they killed her. But I couldn't think about that. If Celeste and her helper wanted to kill Kai, they could have done it there; they didn't have to move her to a different location.

Only through sheer determination was I able to calm myself enough to appear non-threatening. I needed to seem relaxed if I wanted to be freed from my binds and pursue my woman.

Thinking of her beautiful face made me feel better. I could picture her sharp blue eyes, cutting with a look. Her chin raised, and her platinum blonde hair blowing in the wind. A scowl rested on her kissable lips. Yes, visualizing her brought me the level of peace I needed right now because I knew that wherever she was, she would be giving Celeste hell.

"How do we get her back?" I asked.

Thirty-Six

KAI

A throbbing pain wakes me up. The injury to my shoulder hurts more than it has in days. There's a faint scent of blood in the air, and from the wetness of my shirt, I believe it's coming from my shoulder. That bitch Celeste better not have ruined my stitches. If I have to have them redone, I'll make sure she suffers.

They haven't realized I'm awake, so I keep my eyes closed as I lie against the wall, my hands bound to a pipe. The angle of my arms, pulled behind my back, puts pressure on my injury.

I am doing my best not to panic about my friends, the people who have become the family I never wanted but desperately needed. Are they okay? I must hope they are. If I had to bet on it, I'd say they got me out of there quickly and retreated.

As I heard their voices, I slowed my breathing, trying to catch what was being said.

"Why can't we kill her?" asks a deep voice. It takes a minute to recognize it in my hazy state, but it becomes clear it's Riggs. I truly thought he had been taken down in the coup executed by his pack. In hindsight, we should have been more thorough about checking since he was aligned with Celeste.

His steps scuffed across the floor as he paced, exuding a restless energy.

Celeste's voice came from the opposite direction when she replied, "We don't want her dead." I could almost hear an eyeroll in her tone. It seemed like she was at her wits' end with him. Perhaps this was something I could exploit when the time came.

"But why not?" he whined.

"Use your brain. If we kill her, Alder will be broken, utterly useless to us. On the other hand, if we keep her, it'll torment him to know that anything could be happening to her. We can use her as leverage; as long as she's alive, she's an endless bargaining chip."

It was difficult to maintain my pretense of sleeping when she mentioned using me to hurt Alder. I didn't want to be used against him. When they contact my friends to obtain whatever they're after, if they ask for proof of life, perhaps I can convince them not to come for me. I don't want to be used against anyone, and Alder isn't the only person they could target me against. Finley is the alpha of Fang, the largest pack in North America. Imagine if Celeste had control over her. No, I need to persuade them to forget about me.

"Well, I'm not the one who will take care of her," Riggs huffed.

A sound of flesh hitting flesh and an oomph from him followed by Celeste saying, "You'll do as instructed, or you will no longer be of use. You are aware of how I deal with those who are no longer useful to me."

It was a threat, if I'd ever heard one. She would get rid of Riggs and not lose any sleep over it.

There was some moaning and fussing from Riggs, but it didn't take long before I heard their footsteps leaving the room. I waited a few minutes to ensure they were truly gone before I opened my eyes.

The room was dimly lit, resembling something from an industrial building. Numerous pipes adorned the wall to which I was tied, while machinery occupied one of the others.

I tested the restraints on my wrists to see if it would be possible to free myself, but they were tied tightly. If I could find the right angle, I might be able to cut them by shifting one of my nails into a claw, but whether they intended it or not, I was too close to the wall to use my hands in that way. Damn it.

There didn't seem to be anything in the room that would be of use to me either. It really chafed knowing I'd be stuck here until Celeste came back to determine my fate or until I was rescued. The feeling of being helpless made me feel like my skin was crawling. No... there actually was something crawling on me.

Moving my elbow the slightest bit was met with a squeak. Oh, fates! It was a mouse. I felt its tail brush against my arm as it scurried away.

Taking deep, slow breaths helped calm me. I hoped that was the only rodent around, but somehow, I had a feeling I wouldn't be that lucky.

With no way to escape and nothing to do until someone returned for me, I was left to sit in the dark with only my thoughts for company. Regret settled heavily in my gut. I should've told Alder how I felt about him. If I didn't get out of here alive, or if Celeste kept me forever, he'd never know that I loved him back.

He was impossible to guard my heart against. Any fears I had about caring for him proved to be unnecessary. All my hesitations felt useless. In the end, I fell for him anyway. It hurt to think of all the extra time we could have had together if I hadn't fought my feelings for so long. Knowing now that there might not be more memories to make hurts. Everything we might miss out on would be my fault. I wasted so much time that we could have spent making happy memories together. Now, with our fate looking so grim, it seems possible we'd never get to make new ones. I didn't want to live my life without him; I wanted to be side by side until the end.

If I had another chance, I'd share everything with him and embrace him completely. There would be no holding back.

Thirty-Seven

LAILA

Schaffer wasn't a bad boss, but we didn't always agree on cases. When he tranquilized my principal, it angered me and felt like the wrong course of action. I understand he was worried that Alder would go into angry sasquatch mode and that someone would get hurt, but I feel there were better ways to handle it.

I've only been on this job for a short time, but it has become clear how much everyone in the Fang pack cares about each other. Their family-like behavior made me wonder what it would be like to be part of something like that. The connection they all share is worth protecting, which is why I now feel wracked with guilt.

Maybe I should have known Schaffer wouldn't have texted. He is of the older generation, and everything is unnecessary phone calls with them. The text should have tipped me off to it being a fake. If I had figured it out, they wouldn't have taken Alder's mate.

On the other hand, how would it have played out if we had been there when Celeste was? I can almost guarantee they hadn't seen one of my kind before, which could have scared them off or made them respond with violence because they felt threatened.

From the scene of the abduction, it didn't seem like they hurt Kai too much. There was very little blood; to me, this indicates they don't want to kill her, at least not just yet.

After Alder calmed down, Schaffer allowed me to remove his restraints. However, since receiving the news, his demeanor has shifted. He's been standoffish, barely spoken, and overly agreeable. This is suspicious.

If it were my mate who was taken, I wouldn't be hanging around. I would have already left, whether I had a trail of clues to follow or not. This leads me to believe he's up to something.

The office is filled with motion and chaos as everyone gets up to speed. The unfortunate aspect of working for an international agency like this is that many of the actual agents are not present. It would be too time-consuming to recall everyone who's in the field, so we must work with those available here.

Schaffer holds a conference call with Finley from the Fang pack but doesn't let us participate in the discussion. We're left to sit in the hallway like wayward children waiting to be called into the principal's office for reprimand.

Twenty minutes later, he comes out of the office and tells us he's reached an understanding with Finley. The pack will assist in the search and be allowed to help when we find where Celeste is hiding out.

All available agents are directed to gather at the pack's compound to commence a search and investigate further.

"Let's get you back," I say to Alder, and without a word, he follows me to the car. How suspicious indeed.

CALLUM

W hen Hadeon returned with only Tyler, the entire house was thrown into chaos. When Hadeon rushed Tyler into the house, we all helped get him seated in a chair. Leora held pressure on his wound while waiting for the pack healer to arrive.

After Finley talked to Tyler and assured him that he would be fine, she went on a conference call with Agent Schaffer, accompanied by Xan and Hadeon. Since I was still mending my friendship with Finley and trying to build trust with the others, I wasn't invited to join. Sitting by and waiting to hear anything was frustrating. I know I'm not the most popular guy around here, but I've become pretty good friends with Alder, who I knew was probably freaking out.

He's always a chill and levelheaded person, but I can only imagine how he would react to the news that his mate was abducted. I know I would be a mess if I were him.

The study door swung open as they emerged from their conference ten minutes later. Finley was the first to stride out, and despite her short stature, the anger radiating from her felt like it filled the entire room. Xan followed behind, offering reassurances about Kai being a badass and trying to soothe her as best as he could. Kai and Finley had been friends for years, often each other's only consistent contact within the pack when my father was the alpha. They even formed their own temporary pack when my late brother Fallon took over and went psycho wolf on everyone, attempting to claim Finley as his mate despite her objections. It was predictable that she would choose Kai as her second-in-command and enforcer when she victoriously ended my brother's life in an alpha challenge he refused to yield to.

Last to leave the room was Hadeon. The vampire showed no visible emotion regarding whatever was discussed. Not surprising, since he was generally hard to read. Despite my efforts to befriend everyone, he's been the most elusive. Never overly interested in conversation, he offers very few pieces of information about himself. I knew he was likely at least a few centuries old and was one of the lucky few vampires able to walk in daylight. Other than that, I'm not sure where he came from or when he became undead.

Sometimes I really miss my brother—not Fallon—he was truly losing it towards the end. I miss Knox. After Celeste left, he chased after her like a bat out of hell. Or I suppose a wolf after its mate. It's hard to believe, but if what he claimed before he left is true, I feel sorry for him. She is wanted by an international agency, but even if she weren't, she's evil and selfish. She used a love potion on someone I'm starting to regard as one of my closest friends. We all hate her, and even if she resolved her issues with the bureau, she wouldn't be welcome here.

Hadeon ordered, "Get the group together in the dining room," and I complied like a good little soldier.

Once we were all standing around the table, Leora started glowing, trying to spread some of her magic. Ry, her satyr mate, put his hand on her shoulder and said, "I know it's hard not to offer help at a time like this, but I don't think the others want you making them feel better right now."

"I'm sorry," she whispered.

If I had magic that could influence positive feelings, I imagine I would have a hard time keeping that locked away, too.

"Schaffer is calling all available agents to work on finding Kai; unfortunately, he doesn't have many local personnel. Too many are out on assignments, and this wasn't something they anticipated. I've offered our assistance, and we've reached an agreement. I made it clear that we would be looking for Kai with or without their help, so we might as well work together."

"They will be arriving in the next few hours, and it will be all hands on deck. I'll show the crime scene to the agents when they get here," Hadeon told us. "We're not happy about it, but Schaffer thought it best to temporarily sedate and restrain Alder until they knew how he would handle the news. They were worried about a pissed-off rogue sasquatch roaming the city, so they wanted to ensure that didn't become an issue."

Everyone was upset about that news. What the hell? That seemed like a violation. Just thinking about it made me dislike the bureau. My tender-hearted friend was going to be devastated when he found out about his missing mate, and the best way they could think to handle it was to sedate him. What utter bullshit!

"Callum, I'm assigning you to watch Alder when they return. He'll need someone to keep an eye on him. We can't allow him to act rashly or run off alone," Finley said.

That's fine with me. I may not be one of the strongest or smartest, but I needed to be useful.

Hadeon cleared his throat, and all eyes returned to him as he began to speak. Everyone needs to gather their phones and chargers and place them on the table. I'm going to set them all up in here in case Celeste calls us with a ransom. Or if Kai somehow escapes and tries to call one of us, you've all received your instructions; aside from that, we're just waiting for information."

We were dismissed and advised to rest, as if any of us could do so while unknown horrors might befall Kai.

Thirty-Nine

ALDER

Since I was released from the restraints, I've intentionally kept my expression masked. If they could see the fuming mess inside me, I'd end up locked up again. My insides feel like they're boiling with the need for retribution. My first priority will be making sure Kai is rescued safely, and then all bets are off. If the bureau doesn't deal with Celeste, I will personally, and I'm willing to bet my pack will be more than willing to help as well. She won't be getting away with this.

The large blacked-out SUV we rode in finally approached the wrought-iron gates that surround the Wimbleton Estate—home. The sight brings comfort, and a heavy sigh escapes me. This is the place I belong, where I am accepted, wanted, and loved. Hopefully, we will get Kai back soon so that this feeling doesn't become tainted in her absence.

Despite the calm exterior I display as I climb out of the back-seat, I accidentally slam the door. Heads whip in my direction, and I attempt to smile in apology, but it likely looks more like a grimace.

Within seconds of shutting the car doors, my best friends flood out of the house. They beeline straight for me, surrounding me with hugs, shoulder pats, and words of comfort.

"We'll get her back," is a common comment from multiple people.

Without delay, Schaffer and Hadeon break away from the group so the agents can see the abduction site. I'm torn with indecision. Should I go see where my mate was taken from us? It feels like the right thing to do, but it would be difficult to witness. Yet, she deserves that much, doesn't she? While I'm preoccupied with these thoughts and rubbing the ache in my chest, Callum approaches me.

"They'll be back in a minute; there wasn't much to see. Let's get you inside."

For just a second, I considered fighting him on it, but I ultimately decided to go with him when Agent Aziz confirmed his statement.

He leads me into the dining room where we have our family meals. There's a tray laid out with pastries and a couple of metal urns filled with coffee and fixings. I suspect that was Leora's doing. The fairy is always trying to take care of us all, and if we don't let her comfort us with her magic, she'll resort to feeding us.

Callum swipes up a white mug from a clean stack and fills it half with coffee and half with flavored creamer. This is definitely not the way he usually drinks his coffee; I've only ever seen him drink his black. When he brings it to me, it becomes clear why he made it that way, knowing my love of all things sweet.

When they said Hadeon and the agents would be back soon, they truly meant it. Two sips of coffee later, they entered the house. I do my best to pretend I'm not affected when they say there are no scents or lingering tracks to follow. They essentially took my mate and left no trace, nothing to lead us to them.

Hadeon recently installed cameras around the property to enhance security. He shows the agents the limited footage he managed to obtain, which confirms the suspects involved in the abduction but provides little else of use.

As the night wears on, the news becomes bleaker with each new piece we learn. Kai's phone is off and unable to be used to track her. Any security cameras near our place or on the way to or from town were all disrupted, so there is no usable footage. There are no credit cards used by either Celeste or the missing alpha, Riggs, the suspected accomplice. Essentially, they have nothing.

When the sky grows dark and the agents call it a night, I'm still restless. All the agents Schaffer brought here, except for Laila, retreat to their homes or a hotel for the night. They will supposedly be back tomorrow, but what's going to change between now and then? There was nothing to find. My soul feels like screaming into the abyss.

The ache in my chest intensifies, and the stress from my lack of progress makes it harder to keep my beast contained. If I don't want to be imprisoned until they find Kai, I'm going to need some help.

"Do you have any of those special treats that you make?" I ask Leora.

She quickly understood what I was asking about and went to get some for me. The little candies contain magic that helps you relax, and they have proven quite handy when you have trouble sleeping. Technically, the use of magic in food isn't illegal, but some people find moral issues with it because it can influence the consumer.

When she returns to the dining room, she hands me a jar full of homemade chocolates. These are the strongest of her influenced goods; the gummies are much more mellow. They will be perfect for my needs.

"Thank you," I say to her as she hands them over.

I lift the lid and pop a couple into my mouth. The chocolate melts and tastes delightful. If I weren't under such extreme stress right now, I would be savoring the experience.

"Did you use that Belgian chocolate as a base again?"

She confirmed my theory with a bright smile. At this point, Laila spotted the chocolate and came over to us.

"Those look delicious," she says as she gazes at the chocolate. "May I try one?"

"Actually, I'm going to eat all of these." I stuff them into my pants pocket. The jar barely fits but somehow manages to slide inside.

I feel like a jerk when I see the hopeful expression melt from her face. If we weren't in our current situation, I wouldn't care about her trying them, but since some people find the magical treats morally ambiguous, it would be better not to give them to an agent of the International Bureau of Magical Enforcement; we've already got enough trouble.

ALDER

Three days. That's how long my mate has been missing now. And yet, there's been no call from Celeste trying to get a ransom, immunity, or anything. It's been dead silence.

After the first day, I took up hiding in Kai's room—well, our room. We only spent one night in it together before she went missing, but I'm more comfortable here than anywhere else.

Everyone is trying their best to sound reassuring, but I notice the looks of pity. They're just as worried as I am. Celeste is a wicked person, and we have no idea what she might be doing to Kai. Or why she hasn't attempted to reach out to us.

It's easier to hide in here, lying on the bed that's wrapped in her scent.

I'm lying in bed, restless after another day without progress, when someone bangs on the bedroom door.

A quick glance at the alarm clock on the nightstand reveals that it's nearly three in the morning. I slide out from beneath the comforter as the banging goes on.

"Hold on," I grumble.

Maybe they didn't hear me because, irritatingly, they kept banging until I got close enough to rip the door open.

When I glare at the person who disturbed me, I'm met with the frantic eyes of Callum.

"Come on! Get dressed and come downstairs now! We've got a lead." He says all of this so quickly that he's gone before I've even adjusted the scowl on my face.

He came here with important news for me, and I acted like a jerk. I'll have to apologize later for my rude behavior. Deciding to do it after I find out what's going on, I quickly dress and jog downstairs.

Noise from the study alerts me that the group is gathered there. When I enter the room, I find all my closest friends huddled around the desk where Xan sits at a computer. The buzz in the air is palpable.

"What did you find?" I ask as I rush around to see what he has on the screen.

He turns it to face me, but I'm unsure what I'm meant to be looking at.

"Why are we looking at your family's Ancestral Grimoire website?" I ask in confusion.

"I wasn't sure if it would work or if she would even use it, but when Celeste first took Kai, I decided to adjust the settings. " I had to download a plugin to use with the site, so it wasn't obvious to anyone else, but I was able to set it up to notify me the next time someone accessed my family's site," he rambles quickly.

"I still don't quite understand what this means," I say to him.

"Celeste and I are the only ones who use the site. The rest of the family is too old-school, preferring their leather-bound books. I didn't even use it until after that incident when Fallon burned down my club and magic workshop. All my books were destroyed then, so I switched to the digital version." He takes a breath. "It was just accessed, and the plug-in provided me with a location from where it was used."

The grin he gives me looks downright feral; if I weren't so preoccupied with finding my mate, I'd wonder if there was a shifter somewhere in his family line. He has that look about him right now- the look of a shifter about to hunt their prey.

"Let's go," I declare, and am immediately met with a chorus of agreement.

"Hell yeah, it's time to get our girl," Finley shouts, raising a fist in the air.

"And make my cousin pay," Xan adds.

He slams the laptop shut, and we all march to the study door. The door opens before I can reach the handle, revealing Laila.

"It's the middle of the night," she says, clearly suspicious. "What are you all doing?"

"We found her!" Xan says in delight.

Forty-One

CALLUM

We took two vehicles to the location where the online grimoire was used. Knowing we had our first solid lead; our hope was at an all-time high.

Laila called Schaffer, waking him up to update him. She got off the phone shortly after confirming that he was sending agents to meet us. The numbers were already in our favor, but it was still nice to know we wouldn't be facing this alone.

As Xan drove, his demeanor suddenly shifted from excited to very serious. The way his aura could change so quickly was one of the reasons the warlock still scared me shitless from time to time. Rationally, I knew we were on the same side nowadays and that I was part of their pack, but he was still dangerous, and it was hard to forget that fact.

He glanced into the rearview mirror, appearing to make eye contact with Alder before saying, "There's something I need to warn you about before we arrive."

"What?" Al asked, his voice hesitant as if preparing for the worst.

"The spell she was examining." He paused as if preparing himself. "She was looking at a spell about breaking magical bonds."

Gasps erupted all around me.

"What kind of bonds is the spell used for?" Laila inquired.

"Well, I can't be certain, but if I had to guess, she was researching how to break mating bonds."

I wasn't the only one cursing at that.

Alder, who had been trying his best to hold himself together over the last few days, threw his head back and roared. The sound was shocking in the quiet of the night and so full of anguish.

Xan's eyes brimmed with sympathy for his friend, as if he shared the pain too.

"I don't believe she'll have been able to use it yet. As soon as I received the alert that she accessed the site, I gathered us all together. Additionally, some of the ingredients are difficult to obtain; she might not have what she needs. Furthermore, the spell isn't specifically designed for mating bonds, so even if she attempted it, it might not work since that wasn't the intended purpose. Try not to worry; I just didn't want to withhold that information on the slight chance that she might have used it."

The only acknowledgment from Alder was a nod and the clenching of his jaw as he gritted his teeth.

I've never heard of breaking mating bonds. Anytime a fated pair finds each other, they have the option of rejecting their match, but once a bond is in place, it's for life—or so we've been taught.

The remainder of the ride passed in silence. Our destination was thirty minutes away, but Xan's driving brought us there in fifteen. I suppose he wasn't concerned about being pulled over, considering we had a member of law enforcement with us.

Xan announced, "We're here."

Forty-Two

XAN

Parking the vehicle a few blocks away felt like a safe bet since we didn't know who might be helping Celeste. We jumped out just as Ry pulled up with the others, parking behind us.

As they got out of the car, I couldn't help but remember the first time I witnessed Ry drive. It was a few months into our friendship, and having never met a satyr before, I was perplexed. My mind struggled to wrap around the visual of hooves slamming on the brake. Remembering the lecture that followed, where I was chewed out for my small-mindedness, fills my chest with fondness. I was naive at the time, but I've become knowledgeable about a whole host of supernatural species now.

Laila's shoulder-length black bob falls in her face as she leans over her phone, reading something on the screen.

"Schaffer is about twenty minutes away, but he could only get three others to join tonight because it was last minute. He approved for us to start; they'll join us when they arrive."

She and Hadeon talked about the best course of action while the rest of us stood silently.

"We're getting her back, brother," I said, squeezing Alder's shoulder.

He gave me a small smile, but he was holding back. He was doing his best to keep it together, yet I could sense his nervousness in the air. I didn't have enhanced senses like the shifters, but even I could feel it.

I vowed more firmly, "We're getting her back. Then we're going to make Celeste pay."

This time, my words seemed to affect him. He shifted his stance, his shoulders higher than before. He nodded, and a light of determination shone in his eyes.

The leaders of our mission decided that those of us who can shift should do so. Their beast forms would be stronger than their humanoid ones. Those of us who cannot shift would do the stuff that requires apposable thumbs, like opening the doors.

Alder shifted into his squatch form, and through the mental link connecting the pack members, his beast was spitting mad. He'd be able to communicate with the others, but it was unlikely he would since his beast was more primal than wolves. What he lacked in words, he made up for in strength.

My mate kissed me deeply but briefly before transforming into her beautiful, strong brown wolf. Callum followed suit, leaving a black wolf in his place.

That was everyone I thought would shift. I was proven wrong when we saw Laila shift.

"Holy shit—" I stopped mid-sentence upon seeing her.

In her place stood a giant dog. Not a wolf, but something larger, more frightening, and a hell of a lot rarer.

Hadeon sniffed deeply before he smiled, a terrifying sight with his fangs on full display. I can honestly say I was glad he was usually so stoic; his smile was dreadful.

"She has an ancient scent," he remarked.

"What is she?" I heard Leora whisper in wonder.

"I've never seen one, since there are only a few alleged to be alive today, but I'd bet my life that she's an Anubis. They're nearly extinct these days, but they were fierce protectors. If you believe mythology, they were tasked by the Egyptian gods with guiding the souls of the dead into the afterlife," Hadeon answered.

"You know what?" I said. "Hell, yeah!" I whooped, pumping my fist in the air.

She was one scary mother fucker, and I was grateful she was on our side.

She let out a growl that, despite its tenor, didn't sound threatening, and I took that as our sign to move out. The others must have agreed because we took off toward the building.

Forty-Three

KAI

The time I've been tied to this freaking pipe is starting to feel infinite. If I were tasked with telling someone how long I've been here, I wouldn't be able to. The room has no windows, and my captors have kept it dark inside. The lack of lighting has caused my mind to lose track of time. It feels like months, but maybe it's only been a few days.

My body aches and craves rest, but every time I shut my eyes, something wakes me up. Once, it was a rat crawling by, maybe checking if I was a food source yet. Other times, it's Celeste and Riggs coming to taunt me.

They take immense pleasure in telling me that I'm stuck here, and no one is going to find me—ever.

Once I'm free, if I ever see these two people again, it will be too soon. Neither of them has left since I've been here. Unfortunately for me, they've even become intimate during my stay at Hotel Crazy Person.

I've seen their sweaty bodies getting freaky more often than I want to remember. I'm not sure if that's one of their kinks or if they simply don't care about modesty. Many shifters don't mind that sort of thing, but Celeste isn't a shifter, and I'm not here willingly, so I really mind having to witness it.

They recently finished another round of their freak fest, and I did my best to block them out. I leaned against the hard, damp concrete, closing my eyes, thinking about all the things I need to say to Alder when I see him again and all the things I want to do with him. And yes, despite my circumstances, I'm determined that there will be a time when we're reunited.

The two wardens are getting dressed when they hear a loud noise from the far side of the building.

"Go see what that is," Celeste orders Riggs, who is only dressed in a loose pair of lounge pants.

He leaves without a fight to do her bidding. It's sickening to see the deterioration he's experienced since we met him at Harrison pack land. His face has grown gaunt, with bags under his eyes, living in this filthy warehouse building without complaint and fulfilling every wish and demand from Celeste.

She also used a potion on him. I've seen her dosing his drink, which makes me think there must be a time limit on how long the effects last. My stomach hurts thinking of how much worse things could have turned out for Alder when he was under her control. I'm thankful to the fates that things never got that bad.

Celeste eyes me from across the room as we wait in silence. Then there's the sound of growling from the direction Riggs went. There are wolves here besides him.

When a roar meets the right air, I know my mate has arrived. I smile a sickly sweet smile at my captor. It won't be long until I am freed.

She seems to realize this is it for her. She runs across the room and unhooks me from the pipe while keeping my hands bound behind my back. Dragging me up, she brings me in front of her. Hiding behind me, she raises an intricately carved dagger to my throat just as the door to the room is thrown open.

Shadows of numerous beings emerge from the door, but the darkness renders it impossible to distinguish among them until they draw closer to us.

All of my closest friends are here for me. My mate stands tall in his wild form at the front.

"Not a step closer," Celeste says, pressing the dagger deeper into my throat.

It nicks my skin, and I feel a trickle of blood starting to trail down my throat.

My mate roars, and chaos ensues.

A blur—Hadeon—moves faster than humanly possible toward us, pushing me from her grasp. Alder rushes to my side, scooping me up in his arms and wrapping me protectively against his chest.

Celeste, stunned and stupid by the unseen figure pushing me out of her hold, just stands there gaping. At the same time, my friends move aside, making way for the largest doglike creature I've ever seen to come forward.

The black dog stands as tall as a human and looks directly at Celeste. As it moves closer, swirls of bright orange move in its dark eyes, making the effect look like burning coal.

The jaws of the dog-like creature drip with saliva as it approaches.

"What the—" Celeste exclaims, but she says no more as the creature's jaws open wide and it lunges. Giant fangs close around her neck, clamping down and shaking.

The dog emits a gagging noise before Celeste's lifeless head is dropped to the floor with a sickening plop.

We stand in stunned silence until it is interrupted by Xan's shout of, "Fuck yeah!"

My friends who aren't shifted also give a cheer.

Agents swarm into the room, flashlights raised toward us, making it difficult to discern their faces for a moment.

I feel Alder shift back, and then I'm embraced in his human arms.

"Why did you have to have all the fun without us, Aziz?" Agent Laramie complains from the doorway.

I gasped, "That's Laila Aziz?" I ask Alder, who confirms that it is her and that Hadeon believes she's an anubis.

We are led out of the room while the team tidies up the mess. I receive medical attention and need a couple of potions for the severe dehydration I developed while being held here.

When we were allowed to leave and were walking through the parking lot, I used my hold on Alder's hand to pull us to a stop.

The others around us appear to understand that we need a moment and keep their distance.

I throw myself at him, kissing him fiercely with all the passion for everything I should have said before now, letting my feelings flow between us.

"I'm sorry. I was awful," I whisper between kisses. "I love you." I press those words into his skin with kisses.

"I love you too," he replies, trailing kisses along the flesh of my neck, goosebumps rising in his wake.

"I was terrified I wouldn't get to tell you," I confessed.

"I was afraid I wouldn't get to see you again," he replied. "I'm grateful to the fates that we have you back."

A throat clearing shattered our moment, and we turned to see a stoic Hadeon standing nearby.

"I apologize for interrupting this beautiful moment, but everyone is complaining about wanting to go home."

We exchange a glance and follow Hadeon to the car, hand in hand.

Ry ended up inviting the agents to our house for breakfast, claiming that everyone had worked hard and deserved some home-cooked food to refuel.

The first thing I did was shower and scrub off the lingering funk from the warehouse where I had been kept. Once I was clean and in comfy clothes, I joined the others in the dining room.

Schaffer tells us that they subdued Riggs over pancakes and other breakfast food. After a mage healer examined him, it was determined that he wasn't in control of his faculties and, therefore, wasn't after us out of his own free will.

Unfortunately, the potion Celeste had repeatedly used on him had severe consequences. When they cleared his body of the potion, his mind didn't appear to be fully intact. He was going to be transferred to a facility that treats magical ailments. It's unclear if he will recover, but if he does, he shouldn't have any ill will toward us.

Xan cleared his throat and told the group, "No more getting fucking abducted. Two of us being abducted by obsessive psychos is plenty." Everyone laughed as if he was joking, but I could see the seriousness on his face.

So far, we had been two for two on things working out well for us post-abduction, but I agreed, no more.

We were all sipping coffee when there was a knock at the front door, and Callum offered to answer it. He was gone only a few minutes; when he returned, he was clutching some papers in his hand, and his face looked ashen.

"What is it?" Hadeon asked suddenly, alert to any new threats.

"It's a letter from my brother."

"Knox? Where is he?" Finley asked, craned her neck to see if Knox was hiding in the hallway. He was one of us; he didn't need to hide, although he did run off after Celeste, claiming she was his mate. That was the last time we saw him, so maybe I'd be hiding, too, if it were me.

Callum swallowed thickly, and his eyes looked sad as he spoke. "He's not here. When I got to the door, it was just a letter lying on the porch with a rock set on top to keep it from blowing away. It's from him. He said he needed time to recenter himself and that he didn't know when or if he'd be back."

Everyone felt Knox's declaration was heavy. But Finley said, "He'll be okay, and when he's ready to come back, we'll be waiting with open arms."

Epilogue

KAI

Three months later...

"That's the last one," I announce as I place the box in my arms atop the stack.

"Now we just need to put everything away," Alder sighs, sounding as thrilled by the prospect as I am.

Over the past few months, we have worked to complete the interior of the cabin that Alder built for us on the pack lands. He allowed me to choose all the colors and fixtures I desired.

The result was a perfect haven: a comfortable, homey space for just the two of us while still being close to our friends. Tonight will be our first official night staying in our home.

"I have a better idea," I whispered, leaning forward and balancing on my tiptoes as I kissed him.

"Hmm, what's that?" he asked with a spark of interest.

"There are only a couple of hours until tonight's bonfire party. That's not enough time to put away all our stuff, and we've yet to christen this place. Maybe we should do that." I waggled my eyebrows at him suggestively.

"I like your plan better," he growled, lifting me into his arms as he carried us closer to the kitchen counter.

With a few swift movements, he had me out of my clothes, my bare ass resting on the granite counter.

After confirming I was a sloppy mess, he entered me in a single thrust. As he worked my body, bringing us both to new heights, I couldn't imagine a better life.

Want to know what comes next?

Join Savanna's mailing list for an exclusive sneek peak into Silver Ridge Shifters book 3.

Join Here

About the author

Savanna Golden is an indie author from Missouri, USA.

When not spending time with her husband and five kids she can be found with a book in hand or exploring #BookTok (on Tiktok) which helped her rediscover her love of reading. Savanna loves reading all things romance and especially adores the enemies to lovers trope.

Also by

Love was the last thing on Finley's mind, especially after the heartbreak she faced a few years prior. But when her best friend urges her to try a dating app, Finley unexpectedly finds her fated mate, Alexander, a mischievous and charming warlock. Little did she know, their love would be tested when a new alpha takes leadership of her pack and threatens to tear them apart. Finley and her band of misfit supernatural friends make it their mission to stop the tyrant and save her pack. With emotions running high and danger lurking around every corner, Finley must decide who to trust and how far she's willing to go for love.

Also by

When Rafael's dying father dropped the bombshell that he planned to give his shares of their co-owned baseball team to his irresponsible younger brother, Rafael knew he had to act fast. But when he discovers that his estranged brother has been hiding a divorce and neglecting his children, Rafael sees a chance to save his father's legacy and protect his future.

Jenny is a single mother struggling to make ends meet after her ex-husband's betrayal. When Rafael, her ex's brother, swoops in with a proposal to help them both, she's hesitant but desperate.

They agree to a marriage of convenience until Rafael's father passes away, but as they spend more time together, they begin to question if their arrangement is truly temporary.